Dancing Through the Snow

JEAN LITTLE

Dancing
Through
the
Snow

Kane Miller
A DIVISION OF EDC PUBLISHING

First American Edition 2009
by Kane Miller, A Division of EDC Publishing
Tulsa, Oklahoma

First published by Scholastic Canada Ltd.
Copyright © 2007 by Jean Little

"Sing Till Sundown" by Eileen Spinelli,
reprinted by permission of John Hawkins & Associates, Inc.

For information contact:
Kane Miller, A Division of EDC Publishing
P.O. Box 470663
Tulsa, OK 74147-0663
www.kanemiller.com
www.edcpub.com

Library of Congress Control Number: 2009922723
Printed and bound in the United States of America
1 2 3 4 5 6 7 8 9 10
ISBN: 978-1-935279-15-0

This book is dedicated to Jan Feduck,
the Children's Aid worker who read it in manuscript
and told me she loved it,
and to all those caseworkers and foster parents
who work to help children like Min
go dancing through the snow.

– J. L.

Sing Till Sundown

Sing till sundown, hum your joy,
Dress in starlight, girl and boy.
Man and woman climb the hill,
Warmed beyond December's chill,
Reeling, clapping, touch the air:
Is that fragrant music there?
Come the glory, gone the gloom:
In a wondrous huddled room.
Christ the Word we've longed to know
Calls us dancing through the snow.

Gladness deepens into grace,
Weaves its light on every face.
Let us wake the sleeping earth,
Celebrate the sweetest birth,
Pierce the night with festive cry,
Bloom in colors of the sky.
Bring the flute, the tambourine,
Wave the branch of evergreen.
Lost we were a grief ago,
Now we're dancing through the snow.

Eileen Spinelli

Contents

1

In the Recycle Bin

MIN RANDALL SAT ON THE BENCH next to the Royal Bank parking lot and wondered how much longer Enid Bangs, her foster mother, would spend in the bank.

"Don't you move a muscle until I get back," she had said as she bustled away.

But Min was cold. She hugged herself and wondered why old Enid had not let her come inside as she usually did. Trying to distract herself, she looked around the square. New snow was floating down in great, cottony flakes, just right for a December afternoon. A breeze set some of them spinning in a momentary dance and she began to smile. Then a cold finger of wind slid deep inside her coat collar and touched her neck. It made her shiver and blew out her smile. She huddled deeper into her jacket, but it was too thin to help.

The snowflakes were blowing onto the happy-family statue

that rose up from the middle of the fountain across the street. The water had been turned off for the winter, but the statue still stood in its place.

As usual, the stone father supported the mother and she, in turn, held the baby high above her. All three were stark naked. Min, who was growing colder by the minute, felt sorry for them.

Maybe nude statues looked fine in Italy where Michelangelo's *David* stood. The Art teacher had shown them a photo of him and he looked fine. Tall, bare and beautiful. But here in mid-winter in Ontario, Min felt, even a stone family needed some protection from the biting wind.

In her mind, she dressed the grown-ups in ski outfits and put a snug snowsuit on the baby. They looked much less miserable.

But that was not all that was wrong. The mother had the child perched high up on her hands but was not holding on to him properly. If he were made of flesh and blood, he would have given one wriggle and hurtled head over bare heels into the fountain beneath. Even if he sensed his danger and stayed absolutely still, a blast of wind would surely have toppled him to his death.

"Get a grip, lady," Min whispered to the mother. Then she grinned, catching the double meaning in her own words.

If the three of them were alive, Min knew the Children's Aid would have rescued that poor little kid and placed him in foster care. She should know. In her own years as a ward of the Children's Aid, she'd met plenty of babies taken from parents who hadn't looked after them properly.

The stone parents never abandoned their baby, though. There were always the three of them, sticking together, belonging. Even though the little guy didn't have a stitch on, he'd probably fight to stay with his mum and dad regardless of the gusts that buffeted his small body.

Despite her winter clothing, Min felt frozen to the bone by now.

She glanced over at the bank, wishing Enid Bangs would move it. At this rate, Min would be an ice sculpture before the woman reappeared.

Then a piercing shriek ripped through the quiet of the winter afternoon.

"Catch her, Tobias!" she heard a woman's voice shout.

Min jerked around just in time to see a small girl in a scarlet snowsuit pelting past her down the sidewalk. She was heading straight for the busy street that cut across the square at the end of the block. Then the traffic light facing the oncoming cars turned green. People bent on last-minute shopping were driving bumper to bumper – searching for parking spaces, not watching out for runaway children. This one was so short that her head might not show above the hood of a car.

The little girl looked back over her shoulder. Then she gave a triumphant laugh and sped on, straight for the street.

Min sprang up, dashed forward and caught hold of the child by one arm.

"No!" the small girl bellowed at her. "Let GO!"

Instead, Min tightened her grip. The child squirmed and fought like a tiger to free herself, but Min's hold did not loosen, despite the painful kicks aimed at her legs.

"Cut that out, brat," a boy's voice roared.

Then he was there, catching hold of the child by her other arm and the flying hood of her coat.

"Thanks a million," he panted. "Grace has no sense at all. You probably saved her life. She thinks she's Superbaby, don't you, Grace?"

At that, the girl looked past Min, switched off her glare, stopped kicking and smiled sweetly at a woman who came panting up to them. She was towing another little girl by the hand. Even if her clothes had not exactly matched Grace's, Min would have known, at once, that they were identical twins.

"Hi, Mummy," Grace said, innocent as an angel.

"Sweetheart, you could have been killed if Tobias hadn't caught you," the mother wailed, reaching her spare arm to give her daughter a shake, which became a hug.

"I'm not the hero. She is," growled the boy, pointing at Min. "She snatched your Gracie out of the jaws of death and even managed to hang onto her until I got there."

"Thank you so much," the woman said, turning her wide blue eyes to gaze at Min.

Min opened her mouth to say it was nothing, and then changed her mind. She might really have saved the child. It made her shiver just thinking of that happy little girl dashing into the street and being squashed flat by one of the city buses now pulling in around the square.

"You should be careful, Grace," she heard herself scolding like a prissy grown-up.

"Tell Maggot too," the child ordered.

"She means Margaret – the other twin," Tobias explained, doing his best to hide a grin. "Margaret wasn't trying to get herself run over, Grace. Only you."

Despite her own urge to smile, Min too kept her face straight. She said solemnly, "Of course Margaret should be careful too."

"But I *am* careful." Margaret spoke up for the first time. "I am, aren't I, Mummy? Toby let go of Grace and she ran away, but I didn't, did I, Mummy?"

She sounded so smug that Min decided she liked Grace much better in spite of her wickedness.

"That'll do, Margaret," the woman said. Then, to Min, "Thanks again, dear. I don't think I caught your name."

She studied Min with eyes that had lost some of their earlier warmth. Min guessed this lady did not like her darling Grace being scolded by a stranger.

"I'm Min," she said.

"Well, Min, we are very grateful. But I think Grace has held center stage long enough. We must go. Come, children." The woman spoke crisply, cutting short any further conversation.

Min was startled by her tone. If Grace's brush with danger had shaken her mother, she had sure made a speedy recovery. She was now clearly impatient and she rapped out her orders in a no-more-nonsense voice.

Min resented, on the boy's behalf, her lumping him in with "the children." He looked at least twelve. It was also obvious, from the way his mother frowned at him, that she accepted as a proven fact that he was somehow to blame for Grace's escape. It was not fair. Holding onto Grace was like trying to clutch an oiled eel. She sent the boy a sympathetic glance and won a quick wink in return.

"Bye, Min," Grace sang out, all Min's sins forgiven.

"Bye, Houdini," Min said softly as she watched the four of them walking away. They all had a hand to hold, even Tobias.

He had called her a hero. She wished Laird Bentham, the worst bully at school, had heard that. Laird was forever taunting her with the names "Litter-Bin Min" or "Minnie McDumpster." His taunting kept the old story alive. He made a point of telling every new kid about her being abandoned in a washroom at the Canadian National Exhibition. And he always did it where no teacher could hear.

Just the thought of him made her stomach hurt. His family had moved somewhere else a couple of months ago but, by the time he was gone, the damage had been done. She'd be Litter-Bin Min forever.

Forget him, she told herself, and yanked her thoughts back to Grace and her family. Their closeness was what the sculptor who made the statue had been trying to catch, she thought. They were like those people – except that no carved stone could capture the picture that their live, loving family made. Hearing the little girls' laughter, she at last let her own smile out of hiding and wondered how it would feel to have relatives who cared. Did Grace ever stop to think how lucky she was? No. Lucky kids took love for granted.

She could still see them. They stood waiting for the light. Tobias had dropped Grace's hand and taken a step away, separating himself from the other three. Maybe they weren't quite the perfect family she had imagined.

Min continued to gaze after them, entranced. The mother and her twins were beautiful with their golden hair and blue eyes. The boy was paler, so fair he made you blink. He didn't seem to belong with the other three somehow. When the mother talked to him, she used a different voice.

She sounds more like his nanny than his mum, Min thought, puzzling over what was missing.

How would you know how loving families behave? she asked herself, mocking. So far, you have loved nobody and nobody has loved you. You weren't even given up for adoption, you were just thrown away.

Automatically, she reached for the long, thick braid that dangled down her back, and pulled it forward. Holding onto it always gave her strength. Since that day eight years before when she had been robbed of her soft curls, she had fought tooth and nail against having her hair trimmed even a little.

Finally, Mrs. Willis had told her various foster parents to give up the struggle.

"As long as she takes care of it herself," Min had heard her saying. "After all, it *is* her hair."

She had learned to wash it in the shower and patiently comb out the snarls. Then she re-braided it before she left for school. That kept it from becoming a tangled bush. Its weight had long ago pulled straight the soft curls she had had when she was small. Shirl, the woman who had abandoned her, had cut them off as a final act. She now guessed the woman had been trying to change her appearance so Bruno would not be able to find her. But, at the time, she had felt terror and shame as the scissors sheared off her soft ringlets.

"Curlylocks" she had been called now and again, and the Avon lady who had come to the door had said to Shirl, "What I wouldn't give for hair like that! Your little girl is a doll."

"She's not mine," Shirl had snorted, but Min still held onto the memory of the casual compliment. The thought of anyone snipping off even the split ends had maddened her. Ever since her hair had grown long enough to braid, she had withstood all the nagging and even refused bribes.

I was as pigheaded as Grace, she thought, grinning and leaning forward to see if the child was still there. But they had vanished. Shrugging away a lost feeling, she went back to remembering the battles over her hair. Mrs. Willis had been her sole supporter. Perhaps it was because she was the only one who had seen the almost bald little girl the day she was delivered to the Children's Aid office eight summers before. "Here's the kid somebody left at the Ex yesterday," the man who had driven her had said, pushing Min ahead of him into her office.

"They found an address written in her shoes. I guess that's what made her your problem. She told them her name is Min. They said they'd let you know she was coming."

"They did call. Thank you. But she's not a problem, are you, Min?" Mrs. Willis had said quietly, crouching down so that their faces were on a level. "I think you and I are going to be friends."

Min remembered that moment clearly. She had stored it away even though outwardly she had stood like a block of cement, giving no sign she had heard. She had been waiting for whatever would come next, a slap or a stream of unanswerable questions. Her short life had taught her not to trust adults. Bruno, the man with whom she had lived ever since she could remember, had often smiled at her just before "teaching her a lesson" by locking her in the dark closet. She had never been told what she had done to deserve such punishment or what she could do to keep it from happening again.

The driver had shrugged. "Rather you than me," he had said. "I couldn't get a word out of her."

She knew now that Mrs. Willis remembered that meeting too. Recently she had given Min a copy of the newspaper article about the women finding her abandoned at the

Exhibition. It had a picture of her, a tiny, almost bald girl with huge empty eyes. Staring at the photograph of that little Min with her cropped head and blank gaze had made Min understand, for the first time, why Mrs. Willis stuck up for her the way she had.

When the two of them had gone out for supper together that first night, Sybil Willis's steadfast kindness had wakened a faint spark of answering warmth in Min. She had found herself able, at last, to give the briefest of answers to such questions as, "Would you like ketchup, Min?" Ever since that night, Min could not remember her being unkind or impatient. Only tired sometimes.

Min slid off the bench and went to peer through the glass door of the bank to see what was keeping Enid. There she was – third from the front in a long lineup. Min slipped away, before she was spotted, and jogged back to the bench, trying in vain to warm herself. Attempting to take her mind off the cold, she called up more memories.

Mrs. Willis had also happened to be there many months later when Min's first foster mother, Robin Randall, had said, "Would you like a pigtail, Min? I think your hair's long enough at last for a short one."

Delight had brimmed over inside Min, and her face had lit up with it.

"That means yes," Robin had said, smiling.

The instant Robin had finished tying the slim ribbon on the end of the stubby braid and let it go, Min's hand had shot back and gripped the braid in her fist. She had refused to let go. Over the years, Sybil Willis had bought Min a collection of hair clips, scrunchies, barrettes and ties of every sort. Min still had them all hidden away in an old candy box she had rescued from a wastepaper basket in her second-last foster home. When she had followed Enid Bangs to the waiting van, she had silently shoved the box into the outside pocket of the backpack that held most of her clothes. Mrs. Willis has always understood, Min thought, looking back. But how would she feel about being forced to find her another placement so close to the holidays – if that was what Enid had in mind? Wouldn't it be the last straw?

The word *Christmas* slammed into Min like a bulky kid on a runaway skateboard. Carols had been playing in a nearby store all the time she had been waiting on the bench, but she had been too busy with her own thoughts to take them in until now. Then a child soprano began to sing, "Away in a manger, No crib for a bed …"

Min sprang up and then sank down again. There was nowhere to go. She glared at the world around her. She longed to flee. A month ago, when the first Christmas stuff was appearing in every store, she had wondered how she and her present foster parents would survive the holidays together now that the two little Keating brothers who had been fostered along with her had been adopted at last. They had been taken to their new home ten days ago, just in time for them to adjust to having a new family at Christmas.

Enid Bangs had doted on the brothers. Their presence had served as a buffer between her and Min. Min had never been allowed to get close to the little boys, but she did feel the emptiness their going left behind.

Right after they had gone, she had heard Enid trying to get an appointment to see Mrs. Willis. Clearly, the person who took the call had asked Enid what it was about, but she had said she would wait until Mrs. Willis, who was home with the flu, returned.

Before the receiver was back in its cradle, Min had guessed the truth. Enid might say she wanted a temporary break from being a foster mother, but really, she wanted to be rid of Min. They had never gotten along. Min had been shifted before. The Bangses were her fourth set of foster parents. Only with Robin Randall, her first foster mother, had everything gone beautifully – until John Randall's job took him out of the province and Min had been placed with the Edwardses. Then it had been the Snyders. But the break had never happened just before Christmas. It seemed wrong.

Mrs. Willis had not made it back to work until today. During the ten days they had waited, Min had felt the tension building inside her as the time crawled past. She was grateful to have school to go to while it lasted, and she stayed there as long as possible, claiming to be working on research for a project due in January. When the holidays began, she sought refuge in the public library instead.

This afternoon, when she had come in, she had found her

bed stripped of its sheets and most of her belongings jammed into a battered suitcase and the large backpack that had come with her to this foster home. Even the two posters Mrs. Willis had given her had been taken down.

Enid Bangs had stuck her head in at the door and swept a satisfied glance over the bare room. "We have an appointment with Sybil Willis at five," she said. "You'd better take anything else that's yours along in case she has a new place for you to move to tonight. Hurry or we'll be late. I have to go to the bank on the way."

Min thought of asking if she was coming back after the holidays, but there was no point. She waited to see if Enid would tell her or make excuses. She didn't. She didn't even pretend she was sorry.

Perched on the edge of the bare mattress, Min looked up into the stolid face and longed to punch her one. But she knew Enid Bangs would tattle to Mrs. Willis. It would not be worth it.

Then Min realized she had a better weapon that would be safe to use.

"I'll bet Jerry and Jordan are loving their new home," she said softly. "It's great, isn't it, that they have a real mum and dad to love them at last?"

She saw the thrust strike home.

"They were happy with me," Enid Bangs had said, turning her back and charging into the bathroom. Min had heard her grab a fistful of tissues and blow her nose like a trumpet.

13

Min grinned. Then she shrugged off the memory of that small triumph and thought of their upcoming visit to the Children's Aid office. Mrs. Willis had once told her, "Not one of your moves has been your fault, Min. We'll find you the perfect placement yet." Would she understand that this time, too, Min had done her best even though she and Mrs. Bangs were always at odds?

Enid Bangs hustled up to Min now, stuffing some bills into her handbag and starting to lead the way across the parking lot. "Come along, Minerva, or we'll be late."

My name is not Minerva, Min thought for the millionth time as she rose again. "Coming," she said flatly, and started to round the bench.

Coming and going, she muttered inside her head. That's the story of my life. Coming and going and going and coming. Not that I care.

But she knew she lied.

2

Kidnapped

"COME ON, CHILD. MOVE!" Enid Bangs snapped.

Min pushed her heavy feet in an attempt to go faster. They still dragged. She dreaded arriving at the office and seeing pity in Mrs. Willis's eyes. Or, even worse, impatience.

"I'm back in the recycle bin," she muttered, too low for any ears but her own to catch.

Although Enid Bangs was not watching her, Min kept her face blank just in case Enid turned her head. No way did she want the woman to glimpse the rage and despair boiling up inside her and have a chance to nag.

She was almost at the van when a voice called to her from the door to The Bookshelf.

"Hi. Where are you two off to?" Dr. Jessica Hart inquired.

Her smiling dark eyes met Min's as Enid Bangs explained

grudgingly that they were going up to the Children's Aid office.

"We can't stop," Enid finished. "She's already staying after hours on our account."

Min saw the doctor's friendly smile change to a searching glance that measured the two of them up. Min loved those dark eyes. They were so caring after Enid Bangs's hard blue stare. *What's wrong, child?* they asked silently.

Min's eyes lifted to hers and cried out, equally silently, *Help! Help me.*

Min's shoulders were hunched and her thin face stayed locked and shuttered, allowing no smile to surface, no tears to brim over. Would Dr. Jess see? Min knew of no way she could help, but something inside her ached for a miracle. If anyone was a miracle worker, it would be this woman.

Enid Bangs was still blathering on about how late they were. Blah, blah, blah! Min sneered. But it didn't help.

"I'm going that way myself. I have to drop something off at the hospital. So I'll be right behind you," Dr. Hart said. "Say hi to Sybil for me. Hang in there, Min."

Her voice was low and a bit husky. Min liked the sound of it. The woman had pulled off her mittens and her strong brown hand reached out to grasp Min's shoulder. Enid Bangs scowled at the gesture, but the sure touch steadied Min. She knew somehow that the doctor had caught her silent appeal. She felt slightly less alone as she climbed into the back of Enid's van and buckled her seat belt. It was as though she and

16

Dr. Jess were true friends. She had felt it ever since that night she had been in the hospital with pneumonia. The intravenous needle in her arm and the ache in her chest had kept her awake. A nurse had bent over her, decided she was asleep and gone to check on another patient. Min, alone and afraid, had moaned softly. The next moment, she had heard someone speak gently next to her bed. "What's the trouble, little one?" the voice had asked.

Min had opened her eyes a crack and seen a tall woman smiling down at her. She had closed her eyes again and lain and waited. Then the woman, who she later learned was Dr. Jessica Hart, began to sing, her song driving away the terror that had gripped Min.

The woman's long black hair had been tied back with a leather thong at the nape of her neck. It had reminded Min of her own hair, which was growing long even then. She had drifted off to sleep listening and, the next morning, had wondered if she had dreamed the whole thing.

Now she let go of the memory and climbed into the van. She braced herself for the upcoming appointment. When they got there, she hefted her backpack and slung it over her shoulder. Enid Bangs noticed but made no comment except to give a small snort.

"At last," she muttered as they entered the Children's Aid building on Delhi Street. As they headed for her caseworker's office, Min suddenly saw that Enid Bangs was biting her lip and her forehead was damp with sweat. Maybe she, not Min, was the one who had failed, and she knew it. Could she be afraid Mrs. Willis would blame her for giving up on the kid she had agreed to foster?

Min looked away, but she could not feel any real pity for a woman she knew had disliked her from the start. Instead, she felt sorry for herself, faced with one more painful discussion of all the ways she had failed.

The receptionist in the outer office, who usually sat glued to her computer terminal until you spoke, was absent, and the computer was shut down. They went on into Mrs. Willis's waiting room and seated themselves. It, too, was empty. Min and her foster mother waited in silence, not looking at each other or making conversation. All the other staff must have left for the day because the place, which was usually full of people laughing, arguing, talking in hushed voices or making new appointments, was eerily silent.

Although she could not catch the words, Min could hear Mrs. Willis talking to someone on the phone. Finally she stopped and, a couple of minutes later, opened her office door and beckoned them in.

"Wait here, Minerva," Enid Bangs ordered, as Min got ready to rise. "I need to talk privately with Mrs. Willis."

"My name is not Minerva." Min actually mumbled the words aloud this time.

Nobody heard. She sat back down and watched Enid Bangs plod across the carpet into the office. Before she vanished, Min noted a blotchy flush spreading over the woman's plump cheeks and knew that, in the next few moments, she would start bawling.

Min herself despised people who blubbered. Crying let your guard down and made you easier to hurt. As the door banged shut behind the two women, Min set her jaw and sat, waiting for the pair to come out and reveal what they had decided to do with her next. Pressing her feet flat on the floor, she reached back automatically for the comfort of her braid. Her back was rigid, as though she had been carved out of stone like the family downtown. Or wood maybe. A totem-pole girl. But the thick rope of hair she clutched was warm and soft – and hers.

Although she was alone in the room, her face kept its guarded expression. She wasn't about to let what was going on inside her show on the outside. *What are you thinking?* her teachers and foster parents had constantly demanded.

Nothing, she had answered over and over again, her voice flat, her secrets locked away in a box for which she held the only key.

Why should she tell? She knew, from bitter experience, that confiding in anyone was dangerous. No adults could resist sharing your confidences with their trusted friends. Even if they promised to keep quiet, they clearly believed that breaking their word to a child did not count.

To pass the time, she stared at the holly wreath hanging on Mrs. Willis's door and the row of handmade tissue-paper snowflakes tacked up across one wall. Some were carelessly cut out and not at all pretty, but a few were delicate. She studied these few, convinced she could do better if she chose to. But why should she? Nobody had ever invited her to make such a pretty thing. All the dumb decorations told her was that Christmas was coming close.

Min's face grew even stonier. No matter where she was, Christmas would be awful – as usual.

Behind the door, she could now hear Mrs. Bangs's voice, shouting!

Min bit her lip. If only Mrs. Willis would not try to get her to explain what had gone wrong this time. The true answer would be that Enid Bangs and she had rubbed each other the wrong way from the word go, but old Enid would never admit such a thing. When they were introduced and Min had not returned the woman's smile, she had covered up her feelings at once with an even wider smile and a tight hug. Min had not pulled away. She had simply stood stiffly while the stranger squeezed her against her bulging front.

Enid Bangs had been the one to back off. "Well, you're a cool customer, I must say," she had said, with a loud laugh that was meant to hide her annoyance.

Min was not fooled. "I don't like being touched," she had stated baldly. She knew it would sound rude, but she hoped to ward off future embraces.

"My, my, we'll see what we can do to change that," the woman had said, with another too-hearty laugh. "I'm a strong believer in hugging."

Min knew then and there that it was going to be bad. This woman had declared war. She would soften Min up or die trying. When their eyes met, it was like the first clash of swords in a duel. And now, after nearly a year of fencing, Min had won. After all, Enid had just marched into Mrs. Willis's office to surrender, hadn't she?

But she would not admit she was beaten, not Enid Bangs. What lies was she telling? Min wished she had insisted on going in with her.

Then something banged against the other side of the office door and accidentally sprung the latch. Min stared at the narrow line of light now showing. She held her breath. Would either of them notice? No. Min rose, without a sound, and sat down on the chair right next to the door. She had been told that eavesdropping was bad, but how else could she know what was being said about her? Nothing good, she was sure. She wanted to be ready to defend herself if necessary.

Even though she knew they must be discussing her, Min's head jerked up like that of a startled deer when the first thing she heard was her own name.

"I understand that Min needs a place to stay while you go out west to visit your sick mother, but I don't understand why you seem unwilling to take her back when you return. You yourself admit she does not lie or steal or talk back or run away or wet the bed or refuse to help with chores. She sounds almost too perfect," Mrs. Willis said in a sharp voice. "Those are the usual reasons I am given when a child is returned here."

"She's *hard*. You can never tell what she's thinking," Enid Bangs whined. "And she's sly. Ralph feels it too. We can't get close to her whatever we do. I don't know how to explain, but I do know we have done our best, and we cannot go on fostering that child."

"Keep your voice down, Enid. She's just outside. You know we do not shift children without cause. You must be a little more specific. I'll have to fill out a report." There was a moment of tense silence. Min could hear her foster mother starting to huff and puff like the Big Bad Wolf. When she began to snuffle, Min's lip curled. Turning on the tears was one of the ways Enid Bangs ruled her household.

"Faker," she breathed.

At that exact moment, the outer door to the waiting room opened quietly and Dr. Hart came in. Without taking time to think, Min put her finger to her lips. Dr. Hart stared at her, her forehead creasing in a puzzled frown. Min pointed and both of them heard the raised voices. Dr. Hart started toward the door. She reached for the knob and then stopped with her hand frozen in mid-air as the two voices came clearly through the crack. "Heartless, I tell you," Enid said.

"That's not true," Sybil Willis replied.

Jess Hart shot another glance at Min's face. After a moment, she picked up the other straight chair and set it down silently right next to Min's. She perched on its edge, clearly ready to move, but waiting for a few moments to check out what was happening. Without exchanging a word, the two of them sat side by side and listened.

"It's as if there's nobody living inside the girl. She gives me the creeps and I can't make it clearer than that. Even the little Keating boys weren't drawn to her. Ralph agrees. We can't keep fostering her any longer, neither one of us."

Min sat absolutely still, hoping that the women discussing her so brutally would not guess they were being overheard. She ducked her head lower, trying not to be noticed. When Dr. Hart's warm, strong hand reached out and silently closed over her clenched fist, Min's spirits rose a little and her face relaxed. Dr. Jess would not betray her or change sides and turn against her.

"I assume you are unwilling to take another child right away," Mrs. Willis said, her voice hot with unmistakable anger. "When my husband ran into Ralph at the supermarket yesterday, he told him you were planning to visit your mother. My husband asked if she was ill and Ralph said she was not. You must bring him up to date."

At that, Enid burst out, "I'm exhausted, I tell you. It isn't just me, Sybil. Everyone knows the child was abandoned at the Ex when she was two or three. No one in her right mind would throw away a normal child in that fashion. She must have done something to bring it on."

"That is enough, Enid!" Mrs. Willis snapped in a voice that came straight from the Arctic waste. They heard the scrape of her chair being pushed back abruptly. "When are you leaving?"

"After lunch tomorrow. I couldn't let you know sooner. I tried to get in to see you last week, but they told me you were home with the flu."

"I was. Where's Min's stuff? I presume you brought her belongings with you if you are leaving so soon."

For five seconds there was no sound but Enid Bangs's labored breathing. Then she spat, her words thick with rage, "She brought her backpack in with her. I've got everything else that's hers in the van outside. I'll leave the suitcase at the front desk. In case you've forgotten, Ralph and I have fostered over a dozen children and nobody has ever spoken to me the way you did today. He will be very upset when I tell him how I've been treated. Now I am going."

"Go, by all means. I'll find somewhere for Min to stay. You can use the other door. I'll say goodbye to her for you. Usually we try to help children find closure, but it seems to me that you and Min have gone beyond any peaceful parting."

"It's not just me, I tell you!" Enid shouted suddenly. "Natalie Snyder told me she couldn't keep her – and they had her for three years. And there was someone before that. What do you suppose the child did to make someone abandon her?"

"Stop it, Enid."

"I'm sorry, but I'm sure that girl did something to bring this on. It's her own fault."

Her fault … Her fault …

As the dark, heavy words struck Min, she froze. Her eyes stretched wide and her vision blurred. Her throat closed so she could not breathe or swallow. Unable to stir, she waited for the avalanche of hate looming above her to come thundering down.

At the same moment Jess Hart sprang up and flung the office door wide. Enid Bangs, who was standing, glaring at the caseworker, stumbled back against her chair. She let out a shriek like a train whistle and went plum-colored to the roots of her hair.

"Not another word!" Jess Hart bellowed at her.

Min dragged a gasping breath into her starved lungs. Then she stood up and took shelter behind the doctor, who seemed to have grown taller and be about to go into battle for her. Such a thing had never happened before.

Jess Hart did not glance back at her. She was too busy raging at the dumbfounded women.

"Do you realize that you didn't even have the door shut properly?" she blazed. "The world and his wife could have been listening while you spouted all that poisonous rubbish. Min and I have been treated to a real earful. If she were an adult, she could sue you for slander, Enid."

Enid Bangs, looking frightened and furious at one and the same time, was edging toward the other door.

"You don't know what it's like – " she began to bleat.

"Oh yes I do. I was a foster child once and a foster parent too when I was first married." The doctor's answer startled Min. "It isn't easy. But I'm not stopping to discuss it at this moment. Sybil, right now, this very minute, I am taking this child home with me."

"For … supper?" Mrs. Willis asked, her voice weak with a mixture of relief and uncertainty.

Min, peering around the doctor, wished she could give Mrs. Willis some comfort, but she could not think how. She was too shaken herself.

Jessica Hart's towering rage abated slightly as she, too, caught the tremor in her friend's voice. She grinned at the caseworker. "No. I'm kidnapping her. And I have a feeling I might not be returning her soon, even for a fat ransom, not unless she begs me to."

"But, Jess, there's no need for that … " Mrs. Willis started to protest.

Enid Bangs had reached the other door. It closed behind her with a defiant slam. Min could hear her half-running down the hall. But nobody sent a glance after her.

"Save your breath, my friend. Min and I are out of here. You know I'm an experienced foster parent even if Enid doesn't."

"But you haven't taken a child since – "

"Not since Laura reclaimed Toby, and Greg and I went overseas. You're right. But mothering isn't something a person forgets. It's like riding a Harley Davidson. I'll fill out whatever new forms you need, but I am not leaving Min even to your tender mercies now."

"Jess, Enid has done well with other children. I suspected she and Min weren't hitting it off, but had no notion – " Sybil Willis tried to delay her.

"I'm not interested in excuses. Min does not give me the creeps. Enid does. I've been following this child's progress for some time and I've decided we are kindred spirits. I, too, was thrown away in early childhood. And you can tell Enid for me that it was not my fault, any more than it was Min's. Little children are not responsible for the evil worked upon them by their elders. Come on, girl. I've got your pack and we'll fetch the rest of your things from the front desk if Enid doesn't forget to leave them there."

Min tottered as Jess Hart swung around and Jess's hand gripped her elbow and turned her to face the outer door. Before she could say a single word, she was swept across the empty waiting room into the hall leading out.

Min felt as helpless as the girl in the fairy tale who pricked her finger and fell into a frozen sleep for one hundred years. Where was Dr. Jess taking her? But she could find no voice to demand answers. Then a warm flood of gratitude washed through her and started to melt the ice's grip. She still had no idea where they were going or why. But, in the midst of confusion and fright, she suddenly knew, for the first time in years, that she was safe.

And even if something went wrong, and it still might, she had nowhere to retreat to. She must trust her rescuer and forward march.

3

Sanctuary

As THEY STRODE, SIDE BY SIDE, through the empty
building, neither of them spoke a word. Min tried to find
enough spit in her mouth to moisten her dry lips, but her
tongue had turned to a chunk of styrofoam. She felt a jolt
of dread explode within her, doing its best to quench the joy
springing up within her. It shouted that trusting people only
got you bruised and battered.

Kindred spirits. Had she really heard those words?

She doesn't know me, Min cried deep inside herself. When
she knows me, she'll throw me away too. Everyone does. I
have to stay ready.

She turned her back on the woman who had carried her
off, and glared at a piece of paper taped to a bulletin board
near the front door.

With Min's bulging backpack slung over her shoulder

as though it were full of feathers, Dr. Hart marched ahead, leaving Min to come to her senses and scuttle after her. She led the way to her van, still without making any encouraging little speeches the way most new people did. She opened the passenger door for Min. Automatically, Min got in and did up her seat belt. When they were driving down the snowy street, Dr. Hart broke the silence at last by letting loose a crack of laughter.

"Did you see Enid's jaw drop?" she gasped.

Min's head whipped around. Had Dr. Jess actually said what she thought she had heard?

"If only I'd had a camera!" the woman added, still chuckling. Then she caught sight of Min's shocked expression. "I know, I know. I should have given you a chance to say whether or not you wanted to come with me," Jess Hart said. "I apologize. I am apt to get carried away. Everybody who knows me will tell you."

Min struggled to find an answer for this. No words came to help her out.

"You needn't comment," the doctor told her. Her voice was still unsteady with laughter. "I should be sorry, but they made me so furious! I was on the verge of punching that woman in the nose. I bet she prefers toddlers to kids your age who are old enough to see through the sugar coating. Sybil must have been desperate to have placed you with her."

Min had turned her head away again but, at this, it swiveled back. There was a moment of stretched silence before she could recover enough to speak at last.

"She says herself she likes the smaller ones. How did you know?"

"I'm psychic. Let's try to forget her. Min, has it all been too much of a shock? Would you like me to return you to Sybil?"

"No," Min said instantly, wondering what she was letting herself in for. With difficulty, she added, "I wanted to come."

"Brave girl."

They were quiet then. The van headed down the hill and across the river. The doctor drove on through the late afternoon. Snow was still falling in lacy, lazy flakes. The oncoming evening had turned their cloudy white to a soft grey. Despite the islands of yellow light cast by the streetlamps, the dusk deepening into night was strangely eerie and Min, peering out the window, shivered. As they left the center of town and entered the streets lined with family dwellings, she saw that Christmas lights had been switched on in most of them. They passed by others, each more splendid than the last. Min caught sight of a whole team of reindeer on one roof, pulling Santa's sleigh. And a family of sparkling snow people on another. A tinsel-decked troll hugged one chimney and a polar bear in a Santa suit was stretched out along the ridge pole of another house. He looked nervous. Min sent him a comforting wave.

"How silly most of them are," Dr. Hart remarked. "They haven't much to do with the real Christmas, have they? It's just a crass competition among neighbors with more money than sense."

Another silence. Min knew that foster parents hated her silences. She swallowed and forced out one word. "Maybe," she mumbled.

She did not have the nerve to say that she found the childish scenes decorating the houses cheering as they glowed above the dark street. Getting them up there had to have been risky and the people must have been pleased when they had managed it. Especially without falling off and breaking their necks.

Her stomach tightened with nervous excitement. She was certain that she had no need to be afraid of the woman who had just "abducted" her. Once more she remembered what had happened in the middle of that night she had spent in the hospital, the time she had had pneumonia. Her foster mother had thought it was just a bad cold until Min's temperature had shot up and she had grown delirious. Mrs. Willis had been away, and her foster mother could not leave the other children, so someone she did not know had taken her there. It had been like a nightmare. Although people had spoken to her as they started the intravenous dripping fluid into her arm, they were rushed, and nobody had explained to her why she was so sick or assured her that the pain and the rattle in her chest would soon be better. She remembered lying in a high bed with sides like a crib, feeling confused and frightened and lost. When the night shift came on, a nurse had taken her temperature and given her a drink. But, once she thought Min was asleep, she had gone to check on another patient. "That child will wake up everyone if his mother doesn't get him to stop," Min heard her mutter as she whisked out the open door.

Left alone in the shadowy, unknown room, Min had closed her eyes but been unable to keep back the hot tears that slid out under her lids and down her cheeks. Even back then, Min had been known as a girl who never cried, and yet, despite herself, she heard herself moan softly.

That was when Dr. Jess had come and sat beside her bed in the darkness and sung to her.

She must have heard me and known I wasn't asleep, Min thought now. But that night, she had kept her eyes shut and lain as still as she could, drinking in the gentle, healing words.

Goodnight, little girl, good night.
Sleep tight, little girl, sleep tight.
Starlight, little girl,
Shine bright, little girl,
On my little girl. Good night.

It was the only time in her life that Min Randall could remember anyone singing to her or calling her "my little girl." Robin Randall, her first foster mother, may have done both, but that was long ago. The memory of that night in the dark hospital was still vivid, however.

She sat replaying Dr. Jess's amazing statement that Shirl's leaving her in that washroom all those years ago had not been her fault. Dr. Jess had sounded very sure.

Min herself had never known what to think. The question of why Shirl would first cut off her hair and then just leave her in a public washroom had lain like a dark blot in her mind ever since. The story of her being abandoned like that had always filled her with guilty shame. But, if Dr. Jess was right about it, she had nothing to be ashamed of.

Did the doctor know the whole miserable story, though? Would she, like all the others, start asking Min about what had happened?

Now, on the car radio, a reedy voice began to sing "I Wonder As I Wander." Min leaned her head back against the seat and closed her eyes. She felt frightened, all at once, like the child she had been that day, wandering through the Exhibition grounds.

She had trudged around the crowded buildings for what seemed, looking back, like endless years before anyone noticed her. When at last they did, things grew even more alarming.

Two women had paused to stare down at her.

"Are you lost, dear?" one asked. "Can't you find your mother?"

Min still remembered her bright red shorts and the large purse that swung down as she leaned to ask where Min's mother was. Min had not answered. Was she lost? She did not know.

"What's your name, honey?"

"I'm Min," she had said at last. Thinking back, she

imagined how she must have looked with those big eyes and hardly any hair.

Like the little match girl, she thought now.

"Min who?"

She had not known what to say. Determined not to cry, she had stared down at her scuffed sneakers, the pair Mrs. Willis had saved for years and recently given back to her.

The song on the radio went on about Jesus being able to have anything he wanted because "he was the king."

Not when he was a baby, Min thought, her mind drifting. *Snap.*

Min's eyes popped open. The doctor had switched off the radio.

"Are your thoughts worth a penny or are they private?" Dr. Hart asked.

It took Min a few seconds to dig out an answer. "I was remembering stuff," she said.

Dr. Jess shot a glance at her and put her foot on the gas. "We're nearly home," she said. "Supper will help. After that scene in the office, we both need some nourishment."

"Yeah," Min muttered, not correcting her – Jess must have imagined she was still thinking about Enid's leaving.

Really, Enid had only been the last in a long line of people who had left her. "Poor little love," Robin Randall had cried, when Mrs. Willis had handed Min to her. Min had been too tired to speak.

I wouldn't even smile, she thought.

"How could anyone have abandoned such a sweetheart?" Robin had said.

Mrs. Willis had looked into Min's eyes and looked away.

"I cannot understand it either," she had said. "Maybe we'll get some answers when we trace the shoes."

But the address written in the canvas sneakers Min wore had only led them to a woman who had finally remembered being given the shoes by the Salvation Army. When her son had outgrown them, she had put them out in the garbage. They were no help in discovering Min's identity.

Despite this, Min thought those shoes had brought her luck and had been pleased when Mrs. Willis had presented them to her when she turned ten.

"They're a tiny piece of your past," her caseworker had said. "You have so little. They are part of your story and they brought you to me, after all."

Min had tried to say how grateful she was but, as usual, the words stuck in her throat. She came close to hugging Mrs. Willis then, but could not do it. Sybil Willis had reached out and tugged Min's braid gently. "It's all right. I know how you are feeling," she said softly. "I feel it too."

Before she left the Bangs's house, Min had dug the little shoes out from behind a loose board in her closet and jammed them into the bottom of the bulging backpack to go with her into the unknown.

Now Dr. Hart was the future she had been dreading. Suddenly something the woman had declared in the

Children's Aid office rang out again in Min's memory. Dr. Hart had said something about having been a foster child like Min. Had she said "thrown away"? She couldn't have meant it. Not really. Min had never met anyone else who had been dumped the way she had. Longing to ask her about it, Min stole a sideways glance at the woman at the wheel, and then came to her senses and went back to staring fixedly at the windshield wipers swinging back and forth, back and forth. They seemed to be talking. "*You're ... nobody ... You're ... nobody!*"

Min clenched her fists in her lap and blinked away a mist she refused to call tears. When she thought about it, she knew hardly anything about the woman now driving her through the snow. Where was she taking her?

"Here we are," Dr. Jess said, pulling into a driveway next to a low stone house with dark shutters. There was a light on in the front room and, just inside the big bay window, sat a cat who appeared to be watching out for them.

As Dr. Jess turned in, she saw Min craning her neck to keep the cat in sight. "She'll be at the back door to greet us when we get there," Jess Hart said. "She pretends she just happens to arrive there as I come in, but she's always watching out for me."

As the car stopped in the garage, Min reached for the shabby backpack, but Dr. Jess had already slung it over her shoulder.

"Come on in," she said, opening a gate and walking up a

short path to the back door. "We mustn't disappoint Maude."

The cat was a plump calico and, as Jess had said, she was there, come to meet them, meowing a greeting. She wove a figure eight around their ankles. Reassured, Min stooped to stroke her.

"Did you call her Maude?" she asked, just above a whisper. She spoke in a voice none of her foster parents would have recognized. The fact that she spoke at all, without being asked a question first, would have astonished every one of them.

"Miss Maude Motley," Dr. Jess said. "I leave her plenty of food when I go out, but every time I walk in the door, she tells me someone stole it all and she is famished. Yes, Miss Motley, we hear you. Yes, we know you are a fine cat. Yes, yes, a queen among felines."

Min went down on her knees to stroke the butting head with its perky ears. As she smoothed the soft fur, the cat changed its meow into a throaty purr. The rumbling sound vibrated up Min's arm into her body and woke an answering chord. She smiled her first real smile in days.

"My godson, Toby, found this lost kitten on the street a couple of years ago and brought her to me," Jessica Hart said, watching the two of them. "My husband had died a few years before and I had returned to Canada from overseas. Toby told me I needed company. The truth was, he knew his mother would have taken her straight to the Humane Society. Laura does not find strays appealing. Toby calls me Jess, by the way. Why don't you do the same?"

"Okay," Min said, rising from the floor. She must be crazy to feel so relieved. But even though she felt she had known the doctor for years, their new situation had made her uncertain what name to use.

"Good. That's settled. Come this way, Min." Jess Hart hung Min's jacket on a wall hook and went ahead of her into a kitchen. It was a long room with a window above double sinks overlooking the dark backyard. There was an island down the middle where you could cook or perch on a high stool to eat.

"We can start by having some hot chocolate in front of my new gas fireplace, which pretends it's crackling and burning beech logs like a proper hearth," Jess said. "We can have some grilled-cheese sandwiches too. That'll give us the strength to make your bed."

Min could not keep her lips from twitching at the idea of a fireplace playing make-believe games. How long would she be allowed to stay in this warm, welcoming place? It felt like a house in a fairy tale. A hobbit hole maybe. Dr. Hart – Jess – with her long black hair, dark skin and deep-set eyes, was different too.

"That Indian doctor," Enid Bangs had called her. Min had realized, long ago, that her foster mother was uncomfortable whenever they met Dr. Hart or anyone else who was not white. As though she were a foreigner, Min thought, puzzling over it.

Then, one day when Min had an ear infection, Enid Bangs had asked the doctor what country she came from and Dr.

Hart had smiled and said, very quietly, "Canada. My mother is First Nations and my father – well, nobody knows. How about you?"

Remembering how flustered Enid had grown, Min grinned.

"Here, Miss Cheshire Cat," Jess teased as she held out slices of bread to Min. "You butter these on one side and I'll get the cheese ready."

Min bent her head and began. She felt useful and happy. When the sandwiches were ready, Jess had the frying pan hot and plunked them in. The milk for their drinks was heating in the microwave oven.

"What a great team we make!" Jess said, flipping the sandwiches over and giving Min a spoon to use to stir in the chocolate syrup.

"Yeah," Min murmured. She felt her cheeks grow warm with delight.

Enid Bangs, like most of her foster mothers, had made sure Min filled and emptied the dishwasher, kept her own room tidy and did other cleaning chores. She was expected to make her own school lunch – bologna or tuna sandwiches usually – but she had never made Min welcome in the kitchen or taught her how to cook.

Jess, with Maude shadowing her, led the way down the hall to the living room. She turned on the gas fireplace and it did almost crackle. Min curled up on the couch and tried to believe what was happening to her was real and not some dream. Neither of them talked except to the cat. And Jess seemed perfectly comfortable sitting in silence. Min looked around. There were real paintings on the walls. There were bookshelves too and, on top of one of them, two or three framed photographs of children. She glanced at them and then stiffened.

She knew these kids. There was Tobias, looking younger, and Grace and Margaret when they were maybe two. There was another one with the baby twins cradled in their mother's arms. She was gazing down at them as though they were two of the wonders of the world.

"I know those kids," Min murmured. "Is that your godson? Toby?"

"He is indeed," Jess said, turning her head to smile at the pictures. "Where did you meet up with them?"

Min reached to set down her empty mug and it slipped from her hand. She dove to save it even though she knew it had broken. Terror-stricken, she picked up the handle in one hand and the unbroken cup in the other. If only she had been more careful!

"Don't look like that, Min," Jess said, laughing. "I never did like that mug. The handle was too small to hold comfortably. Just be glad you had finished the hot chocolate before it fell."

Min, still horrified at what she had done, sat frozen.

"Even if it were a Royal Doulton cup, my child, it would still only be a kitchen mug, not a golden chalice. Take the bits out to the kitchen and put them in the garbage under the sink while I get out a sheet and pillowcase and a Whispering Silk quilt."

"What's a Whispering Silk quilt?" Min asked.

"It is stuffed with silk from the cocoons made by silkworms, instead of down from goose feathers. A friend of mine sells them. They are lovely and warm and so light. You'll see."

Min did as she was told. Jess had followed her and turned down a hall leading out of the kitchen to the bathroom. The hallway had linen cupboards down one side where bedding and towels were stored.

"The bathroom, by the way, is here," she called as she hauled out bedding.

Min was glad to be shown. After all she had gone through, she badly needed the bathroom. But asking where it was was embarrassing.

"I'll wait for you," Jess said. "I want to be with you when you see your room."

Why? Min wondered. What if she didn't like it? Was it some sort of test?

The room was at the front of the house, across the hall from the living room where they had eaten their sandwiches. It had walls the color of ivory. The windows had Venetian blinds, which Jess closed. They were deep blue. But what made the bedroom different and special was the Tiffany lamp next to the bed. It was dome-shaped and made of many bits of colored glass. The light, shining out through the glass flowers and leaves, diamonds and starry bits, covered the pale walls with rainbow splotches. The lamplight, falling on the bed, was a plain warm yellow, but everywhere else was colored.

The lamp was like a paintbox, Min thought later, when she had had a chance to study it, and the walls were the painter's palette – or maybe the painting itself.

As she stood staring at it, her eyes wide, Jess reached out and gently spun the glass dome so that new patterns blossomed.

"That's …" Min began.

But she could not find a word to fit.

"Enchanting, maybe," Jess said, flipping open the fitted sheet, blue to match the blinds. "I don't know either. When you come up with the perfect word, tell me."

Min reached for a pillow and put it into its pillowcase.

"This room will be your private domain. Nobody will come in here without being invited. Maude will try, of course, but if you don't want company, put her out. She's used to it. It's early, but I bet you're tired out. How about you dig out your night things while I find you a good book to read until you fall asleep?"

"Yes, please," Min said, grateful to have her longing for sleep so readily understood. Feeling shy, even though she was alone, she scrambled into her nightgown and slid under the quilt. She was lying there, watching the door, when Jess returned with three books. Min eyed them but yawned as she

42

did so. Jess laughed.

"You needn't read," she said. "I personally can't settle without a book. I think you'll like any one of these."

The phone rang at that moment. While Jess went to answer it, Min flipped through the books. *Adam and Eve and Pinch-Me*, *The Great Gilly Hopkins* and *Chance and the Butterfly*. She read the blurbs on the back covers. Her eyes widened. Had Jess done it on purpose? All three of them were about foster children!

In the distance, she could hear Jess laughing. She must still be on the phone. Min examined the books more carefully.

Were the kids foundlings? She checked. Gilly Hopkins had a mother. So did Sara Moone. She leafed through the third book. She could not be sure. But the girls were definitely not foundlings. They had been given up, but not thrown away the way she had been. Maybe it wouldn't feel all that different, but Min thought it would.

"All right, all right. Call me tomorrow," she heard Jess say.

What was that about? Min wondered, putting down the books in a tidy pile and trying not to grow tense. It would not matter to her, whatever it was about.

Somebody knocked. Min jumped and sat waiting. Nobody came in. It had to be Jess. She looked at the door, waiting for the woman to come back in.

Another knock.

Then Min remembered. Jess had said she would not come in unless Min asked her to. Feeling foolish, Min called unsteadily, "Come in."

Jess opened the door and entered, smiling. "I thought you must have stepped out," she teased, "or fallen asleep. That was Toby's mother, Laura, on the phone. She's a close friend, has been for years, but she's about to complicate our lives. I'll explain in the morning. You look as though you're half asleep already. I brought you one more book. I thought you should have a funny one." She handed over a copy of *The Prince in the Pond*.

Min stared at it. Without looking up, she managed to ask, "Is it about a foster child too?"

"What?" Jess said, glancing down at the books she had brought earlier. Then she exclaimed, "Oh, heavens! I never even noticed. They're just three of my favorite books. I've met the authors. One of them has been my friend since she was a child."

"Wow!" Min said, startled and impressed. She herself had never seen an author. One had come to her school when she was in Grade Three, but she had been sick that day and missed seeing him.

Jess reached out and lightly patted Min's cheek.

"Sweet dreams, Min," she said softly. "If you have a bad one, I'm right next door. Call me or come looking. I am an expert at driving away nightmares."

Min pulled the quilt up until half her face was hidden. "Could you ... could you sing to me like you did in the hospital?" she asked.

"So you *were* awake that night," Jess said softly. And she

turned out the Tiffany light, sat down on the edge of the bed and began to sing, "Good night, little girl, good night …"

When the song ended, she rose and went out the door, closing it behind her. Then she opened it again. Maude Motley entered, waving her tail, and jumped up next to Min.

"Boot her out if she bothers you," Jess called from the hall. The door closed again. Min reached out to stroke the cat. When she had curled up next to the pillow, Min, taking care not to disturb her visitor, slipped out of bed and went to the window to raise the blind. She wanted the light of morning to shine in as soon as possible. She stood and gazed out through the drifting snowflakes at the streetlight right in front of the house. The steady glow it cast reached right to the front walk. No darkness lurked beneath it. Feeling safe, she got back into bed, pulled up the cocoon quilt, gave Maude another stroke and closed her eyes.

She lay absolutely still, listening to the cat's contented purr deepen into a snore.

Then, out of the blue, a whirlwind of ugly feelings caught her. They were as unexpected as a springing tiger, and as terrifying. She doubled up her right fist and pushed it hard against her mouth. Tears leaked from the corners of her wide, staring eyes and soaked into the pillow. She clenched her teeth and fought to quell the rising storm.

What was wrong with her? Bruno had had no power over her for years. Enid Bangs was not coming back for her. For the first time in her life that she could remember, someone had chosen to reach out for her without being asked to do so. Jess Hart had taken her and, without hesitating, carried her away out of the office and through the city to her home. Nobody had made arrangements to pay her. Mrs. Willis had even tried to stop her. Why was she mad when she should be overjoyed?

Because it can't be *true*, Min shouted at herself. Don't believe it. She will have changed her mind by morning. Don't trust anybody. You should know that by now.

She could not hold back a gulping sob. The cat, startled awake, raised her head to stare. Then blackness closed over Min like a giant wave pulling her under. She went with it gratefully, diving deep into sleep. The bewildering outburst of joy and fury and terror washed away and were left forgotten on yesterday's shore. The evil dream, which haunted so many of her nights, could not reach her. Deeply asleep for once, Min Randall smiled.

4

A Cry for Help

*F*ULLUMP!

The cat, landing solidly on the floor next to the bed,
woke Min. She lay absolutely still, staring around her, trying
to decide where on earth she was and what had made the
unfamiliar sound. Then she lifted her head from the pillow
and looked over at Maude Motley, who was standing at the
door, commanding Min to get up and let her out.

"Coming, Miss Bossy," Min said, and rose to obey orders.

The morning sun was glistening on the heaps of fresh
snow outside, making rainbows even lovelier than those
created by the glass in her lamp. As Maude departed, Min
started to yawn and then stopped to sniff instead. Bacon!

She yanked a sweatshirt out of her backpack, pulled it
on over her nightgown and followed her nose down the hall,
across the end of the dining room into the kitchen.

"Good morning, Min," Jess said. She was still in her dressing gown but the island was set for breakfast for two.

Seeing the careful preparations, Min felt as awkward as an upside down turtle. She had never been in this position before. Was she a guest then?

"Morning," she mumbled, not meeting Jess's smiling eyes. Her own face felt stiff with the salt tears that had dried on her cheeks. She was ravenous, but she did not know what was expected of her. She should have asked some questions before she let herself be swept away.

She gathered her courage, jerked up her chin and forced herself to stop staring at the floor. It was time she found out what this strange woman's plans were. It was so hard, though, to begin.

"What … ?" she faltered, and stopped. Maude Motley came in the cat door and wove a couple of comforting circles around her ankles, purring encouragement.

"I don't know the answers myself, you poor child," Jess said, flipping a blueberry pancake. "You must have guessed that I acted on impulse yesterday. Before we decide what will become of us in the future, I will make you a solemn promise."

She paused a moment and Min looked sidelong up into her face, trying hard to be prepared for whatever was coming.

"I promise you that I will not abandon you. And you will not have to leave my house unless you have somewhere even better to go and you choose to go there. Now, take a seat and have some orange juice."

Min perched on one of the stools, took a sip and tried to say thank you, but her voice would not come past the sudden tightness in her throat. She looked down at her lap and struggled to figure out what was going on inside her. It was partly resentment at being yanked out of one place and carried off to another without her consent, but at the same moment it was also joy at being spoken to as though she would be given a choice before it happened again.

She was relieved when the telephone rang. The jaunty tune it played broke the difficult stillness. Min sat down and went on sipping her juice while pretending not to listen.

"Good morning, Sybil," Jess said, grinning at Min's start of surprise. "Oh, you found someone to take Min. What sort of someone?"

Min put down her juice glass. She had gone stiff as a flagpole.

"A psychiatrist and a teacher of emotionally disturbed kids? Oh, my! That is impressive. Fast work. But, Syb, you must have forgotten. Min has someone already. Me," Jess said pleasantly. "Tell those experts they can have some other needy orphan in plenty of time for Christmas."

There was a pause. Min could hear poor Mrs. Willis's voice, higher than usual, talking a mile a minute.

"What do you mean? Are you accusing me of acting on a whim? But, my friend, we both know I don't have whims. Or, if I do – once in a while – I always carry through. I married

Gregory on a whim and stuck with him. I even made friends with you on an impulse."

There was another pause. Jess was smiling but her eyes were serious. She was quiet again and then she broke in on the other woman.

"I want her, Sybil. Don't tell me you have no other needy orphans. I've met a few myself whenever I've come to your office to see you. How about that little boy with the adenoids and sticky-out ears? They could help him! He'd be just the ticket." Her eyes were sparkling now as she sank onto another of the bar stools and paused to listen again.

Min felt breathless. What outrageous thing would Jess say next?

"Stop shouting, Sybil. After Gregory was killed and I told you I wasn't going back into full-time practice but just filling in for people for a bit, you asked me if I wanted to return to being a foster mother, remember? You were sure I was lonely and you thought a child would heal my hurts. You actually said I'd be perfect as a parent, remember? Of course you remember."

She paused long enough for Mrs. Willis to squawk, and then overrode whatever she said.

"I told you I wasn't ready but, if I ever was, I'd get back to you. Well, I'm ready now and I've even chosen my own foster kid to save you trouble. So what's the problem?"

Another pause. Mrs. Willis shrieked words Min failed to catch. She sounded as though she would like to smack her old friend. Min struggled not to grin.

Jess chuckled. "Such language! I am still a perfect parent, just as you said, sweetie. Min can stay with me for a few weeks or so to start with, and then we'll see if the two of us suit each other. I know that she needs me at the moment so I'm taking a bit more time off. I've never told you the full story, in all its gory details, of my own early childhood, have I? Well, when I do, you will see why Min is going to remain with me at present. You know quite well that I am eligible. Nobody would dream of turning down the noble doctor, so cruelly widowed, so inspiring and wonderful. Now I must go. Min and I have a lot to do today. And we haven't finished our breakfast. Bye, Sybil."

She hung up even though Mrs. Willis was still talking.

"Child, stop goggling at me as though I'd grown horns," Jess said. "How about another pancake or two?"

Min stared down at her empty plate. Her mind was in such turmoil that she did not remember eating the first serving of pancakes, but they were definitely gone. She nodded and held out her plate for another helping while she wondered if she dared ask Jess about her mysterious childhood. She glanced at Jess's face, now sober, and decided she had been nervy enough for one morning.

"You heard all that, Min, right? Syb found a couple willing to take you on and was about to tell me where to deliver you when I said no. She was more than slightly stunned, but I was able to pull the rug out from under her by telling her that you and I shared some ugly childhood experiences. I'll tell you sometime, but not now. We have places to go and things to do."

Min opened her mouth to ask if Jess was still lonely, but caught the words back. She hated being quizzed about her feelings. Jess was telling her so much already.

"What happened to your husband?" she asked instead, keeping her eyes on her plate and speaking just above a whisper.

Jess answered at once, in a quiet, matter-of-fact voice that eased the knot in Min's chest. "He was killed when the bus he was on was bombed. I had just gotten off so I escaped with only a few scratches. We were working in a refugee camp in Mozambique. They sent me home to recover, but I did not go back to the camp, not without Gregory. We worked as a team. Once the team was split apart, I ... Well, use your imagination, Min. Are you almost finished? I have plans, remember."

Min stuffed in her last bite and rose. She stood waiting, excited about Jess's plans, sad about Gregory Hart's death, confused about what was expected of her. "Plans?" she echoed.

"Go get dressed in your warmest clothes. We are going to the country."

"What for?"

"You'll see. It's a surprise. Get a move on."

Min raced into her room and dressed like a fireman called to a four-alarm fire. She had no warm pants, just jeans, but she put on two sweatshirts and her heaviest socks. In ten minutes they were getting into the van. Jess put a saw and a hatchet on the floor in the back. Then they took off, heading out of town.

"Go ahead and ask," Jess said.

"Ask what?" Min's face was blank.

"Oh, well, if you aren't curious, I won't bother to explain why we will be needing a hatchet and a saw."

Min choked. Her polite mask cracked and she grinned. "Why are we taking a saw and hatchet?" she asked meekly.

"We'll need them to cut down our tree."

A silence fell. Min turned in the seat to look at Jess. "What tree?"

"Christmas tree, of course, silly. Start thinking what sort you want. I believe Mabel has lots of choice on her property."

"I don't know anything about trees," Min said.

"Well, I do. But this time, you get to pick. And you can take time to look them over before you decide which one will be just right for our house."

Min found the incredible words echoing around and around inside her head. *Our house. Just right for our house.*

"You mean ... it will be a real tree?" she asked, unable to take this in. They had had Christmas trees at each of her foster homes, but those she remembered had been fake ones that you unpacked and assembled.

"Certainly. Totally real trees. I have never had an artificial tree since I was old enough to choose."

"Is that okay, cutting down real trees?"

"Where we're going, it's fine. The man who planted the trees at Mabel's put them too close together. If some aren't taken out, the lot of them will push into each other and grow too tall and spindly, trying to get more light. You'll see."

Min did not know what to say so she said nothing.

As they left the city behind, Jess said, "I have not warned you yet about the complications we are soon to face."

Min waited, wordless. She felt dizzy with all the complications she had already encountered. What next? Jess wasn't going to break her promise, was she? Min bit her lip and braced herself.

Jess grinned.

"You certainly are a restful girl," she said. "No swarm of questions. No shrieking. But you look as though you are expecting a spoonful of castor oil. It isn't that bad. You remember my godson Toby?"

Min nodded.

"Well, as I told you already, his mother called last night after you went to bed. I understand you saved Grace's life yesterday. Laura told me about Grace's close call, and a girl with a long braid catching her, and I figured the rest out for myself. I remembered you recognizing them in the picture."

"I did grab her, but it wasn't such a big deal," Min said, staring down at her knees. "If I hadn't, somebody else would have done it." She felt her cheeks grow hot under Jess's smiling glance.

"That's not what Toby said. But your heroism was not

what Laura phoned about. Last night, she had an S.O.S. call from her husband's father, about the twins' grandmother. The old lady went to the hospital after having a panic attack brought on by her angina. She's home again but she feels sure she is about to die and she is begging to see her darling granddaughters one last time. Baxter – that's Laura's husband – is already on his way out there. I swear, that man is putty in her hands. So Laura and the girls are flying out to be there in time to open their Christmas gifts with Grandma."

The sarcastic note in Jess's voice confused Min.

"Don't look at me that way, child. This is not the first time this woman has summoned Laura and her girls to her deathbed. So far, she always recovers miraculously the minute they get there. Then they have to stay for a proper visit, of course. I know I shouldn't speak of her this way, but what makes me mad is the way she totally ignores Toby. I'm not quite as heartless as I sound."

"No," Min murmured. "You're not heartless at all."

Jess gave a crack of laughter.

"I don't get it, though," Min said. "Isn't Toby her grandchild too?"

"No. He's Laura's first husband's boy. She and Patrick were divorced when Toby was four. A couple of years later, she married Baxter and they soon had the adorable twins. Toby's dad, Patrick, is a journalist. He roves from one trouble spot to another all over God's earth. He was away and in danger too often to suit Laura. Baxter, on the other hand, is the head guy at a large insurance company and never goes anywhere except to conferences."

"You don't like him," Min stated, and then wished she'd held her tongue. What was happening to her? She, the girl who barely spoke, was talking more every hour that passed.

"I don't *dislike* him," Jess said slowly, thinking it over. "He's kind, and Laura no longer has money worries. He's just a bit flat after Patrick. I like Patrick a lot. He was a close friend of my husband's."

Min waited to learn what the "complication" was, although she thought she could guess.

Jess read her thoughts. "Toby is the complication, of course. He's not going to Saskatoon, so he's coming to spend Christmas with us."

"Oh," was all Min could think of to say.

"Patrick is in Indonesia or Sri Lanka at the moment, I believe, but he's due home on the twenty-seventh. So he'll be with us too. Toby won't mind missing a trip to Saskatoon. He doesn't hit it off too well with his stepfather, and it's tricky for him when Patrick and Baxter are both around. Toby told me once that it was like walking a tightrope. They are very different and he is the son of both."

They were now on a gravel side road. Then Jess turned off and went bumping up a farm lane. Min could see the woods over to their right. She stared at the trees. They were crowded close. She saw no clear spaces where you could walk among them with ease. Maybe Jess was right.

Yet, as they got closer, Min could see that in the woods the trees were alive and they had each other for company and all the bigness of the sky above them with its glory of stars at night and its scudding clouds and rainbows by day. It didn't seem fair to chop one down and take it into a stuffy house and decorate it and then put it out with the garbage when the holiday was over.

"What's worrying you, girl?" Jess demanded as she switched off the ignition.

"Nothing," Min muttered.

"That is not true. But we'll have to talk later. Mabel is at the door, waving to us."

Min saw the woman standing in the open doorway, beckoning to them to come in. She was leaning on a cane.

"She told me she twisted her ankle," Jess murmured, "but it doesn't look too bad from here. At least she's on her feet. I'll have to sit with her for a bit, though, and hear the whole story. Mabel never skips even the smallest detail."

Min shut the van door and then blurted out, "After we say hello, could I go for a walk until you're done?"

Jess seemed to be studying Min's face. Min knew it had gone blank again. She could hide behind that blankness. But should she stop hiding now? Maybe she should try to let Jess see what she felt. She did her best to smile.

Jess smiled back, patted Min's shoulder, and said, "Good thinking. That'll give Mabel and me time to have some coffee and cake. I'll honk the horn when I'm ready for your help."

Min felt a weight lift off her heart. No argument, no sarcastic remarks, no need to invent excuses.

She shook hands with Jess's friend and let the doctor get her out of joining them inside. Then she turned and headed out across a snowy field. She had never been alone in a field of snow before, never been anywhere – except a park or someone's yard – where there was not a sidewalk to walk on. She started leaping, making giant tracks. She stretched out her arms in all the space and whirled around in a dance, celebrating freedom. Her braid swung out behind her and the wind sang in her ears. She felt her whole face shining. She clapped her hands above her head and kicked one leg out straight the way she had seen a Cossack dancer do on TV. Then she slipped and landed flat on her back. While she was down, giggling like a two-year-old, she remembered kids waving their arms and legs, making angels in the snow. She tried it. When she got up, being as careful as she could, the result did not look all that angelic, but she was pleased with the wings.

She tried making snowballs next, but the snow was too dry to pack properly. Her jacket and jeans were damp from angel making and she shivered. Trying to warm up, she set out walking as briskly as the snow would let her. Jess had lent her a pair of kids' boots she had dug out of the back of a closet. They were fleece-lined, but a bit small – her pinched toes already felt like knobs of ice. Every so often she stood still and listened. But no horn called her back.

Then she came to a ruined outbuilding. It was a wreck. Only half the roof was on and the whole thing leaned sideways. It was too full of cracks to keep out much of the December blast, but she stepped inside, grateful for any shelter. Then, as she crouched over, hugging herself, she heard a whine she knew was not the wind.

Some other creature was in the shed with her.

She held her breath and peered around at the dusty wreck of what might have once been a cow barn. There was nothing alive there. There were only some weathered boards, a bucket that was badly dented, a cracked bowl and not much else. She must have been imagining things.

Then something moved.

Min gasped. Whatever it was was pressed tightly into the back corner and it was alive. She stared at it, shrinking with fear. It was some sort of small animal. Maybe a rat.

Maybe a rabid squirrel!

At that alarming thought, she sprang toward the opening she had come through, her breath coming fast and her heart pounding. Then, as she was about to flee back to Jess and safety, she heard the faint, desolate whimper again.

And, in the same instant, the car horn honked.

5

Throwaway Dog

MIN TOOK TO HER HEELS. She ran back the way she had come, sure something was chasing her. But long before she reached Jess's van, she knew no rat or squirrel had made that small, hopeless sound.

Jess, the saw in her hand, stood waiting for her. As Min came close, panting, Jess began to stride across the open field next to the woods. She looked annoyed about something. Min opened her mouth to start to tell about the sound she had heard, but closed it again. She had better wait until they reached the trees and Jess halted. She needed to get her breath back. It was hard enough for her to explain something difficult, without huffing and puffing while she spoke.

"Sorry we took so long," Jess threw over her shoulder.

Watching the back of Jess's coat and noting the set of her

shoulders, Min felt the woman was giving off sparks. She was mad about something, that was for sure.

But she, Min, had done nothing. Please, she prayed silently, let her get over it fast.

As they reached the edge of the trees, Jess halted, took a deep breath and started letting off steam. "Mabel has family troubles she had to tell me about. Every detail! I don't even know them. That woman can stretch a story out until you think you'll go crazy. I told her you must be getting cold and I mentioned that Toby was coming before supper, but she ignored me and kept talking. I'm sorry."

"Oh," Min said feebly.

"Let's go choose ourselves a tree before you turn into an icicle."

Min was so worried about whatever had made that small, pitiful cry that she had forgotten they had come for a Christmas tree. Couldn't Jess see she, Min, was worried? Desperate, she chose the first tree she saw without taking time to study it, let alone decide it was perfect. It was a white pine a head taller than Jess.

"Well done," Jess said with a crooked smile. "White pines are my favorites too. They don't bite the hand that decorates them."

She was waiting for Min to smile back, but Min was not even looking at the tree as Jess bent to begin cutting it down. Instead, she stared into the distance, frantic with worry.

"Your turn." Jess straightened and held out the saw. But

Min stood like a post, making no move to take it.

"What on earth is the matter with you? Take the saw. You have to do your share of the work, miss," Jessica Hart rasped.

Min jerked to attention and tried to obey. She had never used a saw before and had no idea how to put it to use. She did not do a good job. At last, finally, Jess gave a snort of disgust and took the saw back.

"I'll finish," she said. "Then you can put your back into dragging it up the hill. And you can tell me what's got you in such a tizzy."

Silently, Min helped push and drag the pine across the snow to the van. The two of them hoisted it in.

"Okay. Now, what's upset you, Min? Something has. You are acting like a ninny."

Min ignored the insult. "Please, come with me. I have to show you something," she burst out through chattering teeth.

She longed to turn her back on the animal in the shed, but she knew if she didn't get Jess to come and see what was wrong, the stricken creature would invade her dreams.

"But, Min – "

Min reached out with both hands and began to haul Jess along.

"Come," she panted. "It doesn't sound like a rat. Please, just COME!"

Jess had been holding back. The startling words, plus one look at Min's face – usually so blank, now filled with terror and purpose – changed her mind abruptly. "All right. I'm coming," she said, following.

She jogged at Min's side until they reached the ramshackle shed.

"It's in the back corner," Min got out, her breathing ragged. "I don't know what it is. But it whined. I ... I couldn't just go on home without knowing."

Jess moved through the dusty wreck of what had once been a useful building. As she spotted the small heap of filthy fur, she slowed and stared hard. Then she knelt and, keeping her gloves on, reached out and drew the animal towards hers. It cried out and Min leaped back, her face twisted with fear and pity.

"Is ... is it a rat?"

"No. It's a dog. But she's skin and bone. I think maybe she has had puppies. Oh, I don't know. We'll have to get her out of here and take her to Jack."

"Who's Jack?" Min asked.

"Maude's veterinarian. In the van, between our seats, there's a bag of things I was going to give to the church. In it, there's a sweater someone gave me. I think there's a shawl sort of thing too. Could you run back and get them? We'll need something to wrap her in."

Min was leaping back up the hill without stopping to say a word. She ran for all she was worth. The snow kept trying to trip her, but she yanked her feet up like a high-stepping horse before it could make her actually fall. She snatched up the whole bag of stuff and, with it bumping against her, raced back. By the time she reached Jess she was panting heavily and puffing out great clouds of steam.

Jess was on her knees, ignoring the filthy floor, murmuring comforting words to the bundle of matted fur. But the dog's eyes were open now and its tail stirred slightly. Jess had done her best to check on how badly it was hurt, but was frustrated by caked mud and dim light and the small animal's cringing away from her probing touch.

"We'll have to go easy," she said, taking the shawl from Min's shaking hand. "She's hurt. Either somebody kicked her or ran into her or perhaps a large dog got her. I doubt that last, though. A dog would have broken her neck. Here, let's slide the sweater under her."

The tiny dog cried out when they moved her, but she was too weak to fight them. Jess wrapped her in the soft wool, her deft hands making no rapid movements.

"I'll carry her to the van. When you're inside, I'll put her into your arms," she said to Min. "We'll try not to hurt you any more, poor baby."

All traces of impatience were gone. She was the Dr. Hart who had sung a lullaby to a lonely little girl in the children's ward years before.

But Min was not reliving that long-ago time. Every atom of her was concentrated on the job at hand. She was shaking with fright when she held out her arms for the tiny dog. What if she should hurt her more? Did the dog know they were trying to help? She leaned back, cradling the small bundle, and sighed with relief.

"What sort of dog is she?" she asked. "Or can you tell?"

"I can't tell for sure," Jess said, getting in next to them. "Pugs and Pekes both have black faces like this, and she is definitely not a pug. She may be some kind of cross. It's hard to tell through the burrs and dirt." She glanced at Min. "Are you all set now?"

The sun had moved across the sky and it was now afternoon. Neither of them noticed. They drove back to town and then out almost into the country again. Jess pulled up in front of the clinic just as the veterinarian was locking the door.

"Jessica," he said, "I was about to go home to get a bite to eat. Did you need me?"

"Come and see the challenge my foster daughter Min has found for you," Jessica Hart said.

Min was turning carefully toward the open door to let the doctor look at what she held when the word *daughter* made her go still for a second. Her eyes went wide. Then she pushed the moment of wonder out of the way and returned to her small burden. She waited for Jess to open the door wide for her. Then she slid out of the van without relinquishing the bundle.

Jack Miller stared down at the pair and unlocked his office again. "Call my house, Jess, and tell them I'll get there when I can. Min, bring your patient in here."

Min lowered the dog, still swaddled in the shawl, down onto the examining table. Biting her lip, she watched closely

65

as Dr. Miller very gently undid the folds. The dog whimpered and flinched at his touch. Min's heart lifted – the dog might be hurting, but at least she was still alive.

"She's in a bad way," the doctor said, as Jess came back from making the call. "The kindest thing would be to put her to sleep."

"No!" Min shouted, startling them with her intensity. Her eyes and her voice were fierce. "You can save her. You have to try."

Jess put a hand on her shoulder. "You don't want her to suffer," she began.

"If she can get well, maybe she can get over the hurt," Min said. "I've been beaten and thrown away and nobody wants me, but I am glad nobody put me to sleep."

"But, Min – " Jess began.

Min rounded on her. Her face was pale. "We've killed one white pine today. Isn't that enough?"

Their eyes met and held. Then the woman's gaze dropped, defeated by Min's steel. "Do your best to save the dog, Jack," she said. "Min is the decider this time – and she might know more than either of us."

Half an hour later, Min and Jess came out of the clinic. The small dog was left behind. She was warm and dry there and she had been given a shot to ease her pain. Dr. Miller had gently swabbed away the mud from her tiny face. The burrs that were not deeply embedded in her fur had been snipped off so she could be examined better. Somehow this made her look even more fragile and desperately ill than she had before.

"I'll finish cleaning her up tonight," he told Min. "And get an intravenous started. She needs fluids and antibiotics for sure. Maria, my partner, will be back in a few minutes. She'll take great care of the dog. She's a real softie. But the dog still might not make it. She's been badly traumatized. You must face facts."

Min longed to ask him to try his hardest to save the little dog, but she knew he would. Or she thought she knew. She kept her head down as she followed Jess to the van.

"We'll do our best for her, I promise," the man said gently, patting her back as she went by.

Min hated being touched by strangers, but she was grateful for the kindness she felt in his gesture. She raised her head and forced a smile. "Thank you," she whispered. "Try your hardest, okay?"

He nodded and went back inside.

Once they were on their way, Min could not choke back the questions a moment longer. "Is she going to die, Jess?" she blurted. "Is she hurt too badly to recover?"

"Min, nobody can know for sure. But I'll take you back tomorrow and you might put the will to live into her. I've seen children die from a bad case of flu and others get well from something I was certain would kill them. I would think it is much the same with animals. Did you get a whiff of her breath?"

Min's nose wrinkled up, remembering. The dog had panted and the stink that breathed out from her open mouth had come close to making Min gag.

"Jack says he doesn't believe she is very old, but her teeth are a mess. They're all covered with tartar and her gums are doubtless infected. When he gets her clean, he'll be able to check for injuries. I noticed one of her paws is swollen. I touched it with one finger and she flinched."

"Oh, Jess," Min whispered. "How could it happen?"

"Well, today – among many other things – Mabel mentioned that she suspected a couple across the valley of running a puppy mill. Have you heard of those?"

"Is that where they have too many dogs and make them have puppies too often and sell them when they're too young?"

"You have the idea. They neglect the dogs, but use them to produce litters like a puppy factory. Anyway, Mabel said that she had asked some neighbors about them and the neighbors said the people don't let anyone near their property. The man has even been seen prowling around carrying a shotgun. Everyone is hoping they'll go out of business and move on."

"Oh," Min breathed. "No wonder the dog ran away."

"We don't know she came from there, not really. Listen, I think we should remember the reason for our trip and that we are taking home a beautiful white pine at this very moment. Toby is coming over to help us put it up and string the lights. I always have trouble with that part. We'd already made those arrangements before Laura called with the change of plans, so he might come and then go back home, or he might just come and stay. We'll find out when he arrives."

Min made a face like the one she had made when she thought of the dog's foul breath. She didn't like boys. Little ones weren't bad, but boys around her age were nothing but trouble – look at the names Laird Bentham had called her. She opened her mouth to say so and recalled, just in time, that this particular boy was Jess's godson. She probably doted on him. When he made it clear that he did not like Min one bit, Jess, despite her promise, would likely want her to move out. It had happened before. She was used to it. Litter-Bin Min, as Laird so sweetly said, was used to being recycled.

But as she told herself how little it would matter to her, Min felt a soreness, like an ugly bruise, spreading through her. The pain felt new and she did not know how she could shrug it off. Her mouth clamped shut and she looked away.

Jess drove the van into the garage without saying another word. She switched off the ignition. Then, sitting in the dark, she quietly broke the loaded silence. "I think you've been hurt by bullies, but Toby is not that sort of boy. He's not an angel, Min, but I believe, if you give him a chance, you and he will hit it off."

Min could not think of anything to say about such a crazy notion.

Jess waited for a few seconds to tick by. Then she sighed. "Perhaps I should not tell you too much about him – it's his story to tell, really – but you need to know that he was my last foster child. I used to foster babies who were at risk for one reason or another. Toby's like you and me, Min. He began life as a premature baby and nobody wanted him. Well, that is not quite true. Patrick wanted him, but because Toby arrived almost three months ahead of time, Patrick was not even in Canada, let alone holding Laura's hand. Toby almost died at birth. He spent weeks in an incubator and he was the ugliest, scrawniest scrap of a child you ever saw. Laura had not intended to have a baby so soon, and she was terribly shocked when she saw him. Have you ever seen a very small premature baby?"

Min shook her head. Of course she hadn't. How would she?

Jess was about to go on when she saw Min's stony expression. She stopped short, swung open the van door and snapped, "Forget it for now. We'd better get inside and order the pizza."

Min was about to follow her when she realized, all at once, that she had been picturing Laird Bentham. Toby's face pushed Laird's out and Min saw again the wink he had sent her over Grace's head.

"I'm sorry," she began, scrambling out and trotting after Jess, who was striding away from her without a backward glance. "I didn't mean – "

"Let's leave it for now," Jess's voice came back out of the shadows. "We can talk it over later. Just see that you don't hurt his feelings."

"I promise," Min said in a small voice, but she did not know if Jess heard.

6

Toby Again

THE DOORBELL RANG just moments after they hung up their coats.

"Come on in, Tobe. I left it open," Jessica Hart called.

And Grace and Maggot's big brother walked in. He was about to say something when he caught sight of Min. He stared at her, his eyes wide, his mouth ajar.

"All right, Tobias. You needn't gape at Min like that. She is not an alien. She's my new foster daughter," Jess said, her voice sounding too hearty.

"But I know her," Toby said. "She's the girl who kept Grace from running out into the traffic downtown – didn't I tell you … ? No, I guess there hasn't been time."

"Your mother told me a scrappy version last night. Let's fetch the tree in and you can tell me more while we decorate it," Jess said, smiling at the two of them. Her eyes did not meet Min's, but her voice was warm and almost easy now.

Feeling uncomfortable at knowing personal stuff about this boy, Min spun around to go back out for the tree.

Behind her, Jess and Toby began marching along, singing like idiots, "Oh, Christmas tree, oh, Christmas tree … "

At first Min longed to turn and punch them, but, breaking in for the first time, came the understanding that because of everything that had happened since she was at the Children's Aid office, she was going to be spending Christmas not with the Bangses, not with strangers, but with Jess. In one glorious rush, all her jumbled feelings slid away like snow off a peaked roof. She stood transfixed, trying to take in the fragile wonder dawning within her. It was like a sunrise when you were expecting nothing but rain. Or a shimmering soap bubble, floating up, carrying you with it.

She had hated Christmas for years. Her dislike of it had strengthened as each new one came and went, promising so much and breaking the promise every time. It had begun with a feeling of not belonging. And then, bit by bit, it had grown, draining the celebration out of the whole holiday. She knew the exact moment it had started to go bad. All the kids in her second foster home had had bright homemade Christmas stockings with their names embroidered on them. Min had arrived there in late October, leaving plenty of time for the foster family to decide how to include her in their Christmas festivities. But when Christmas Eve arrived, the foster mother handing the stockings out to be hung had suddenly realized she had not got one for the new girl. She had quickly dug out a pair of red nylon tights from a bag that Min knew was meant for the Salvation Army, and given them to Min with a toothy smile.

"This will be just right for you, Minerva," she had said. "See. It is the biggest."

"I'm Min," she had mumbled.

"Minnie," one of the girls had whispered, and they had all giggled. In the morning, while the other stockings overflowed with gifts, Min's red tights were less than half full. And the presents they contained were sensible, dull ones – a plain T-shirt, socks, a large orange and a bag of candy.

From then on, Christmas continued to be the day when she felt like an outsider, from the moment she woke until she fell asleep. Her gifts were mostly donations from the Children's Aid, and were duller and smaller than the family's own kids got.

Mrs. Willis had always given her a book, carefully chosen, with her name written in it. She had tried to keep each of them and had managed to hold onto three. The others had vanished from her room at the Snyders'. She had wanted to complain, but she had learned, by then, to keep quiet. Her silence made the others fear her. She had liked that.

But it will be different with Jess, she thought. Nothing scares her.

And she heard again, deep within herself, the magic

words, *my foster daughter, Min.*

"Hey, kid, move along," Toby growled behind her. "I want to get through with this job before midnight."

Min scowled but speeded up a little.

"As soon as we get it inside, I'll go and get us some pizza," Jess announced. "Do you realize, Min, that you've had nothing to eat since those blueberry pancakes?"

It was true. And the very mention of the word *pizza* made Min's mouth water and her slow pace quicken.

"It's a deal!" Toby shouted, hoisting the tree up onto his back. "Clear the way!"

In no time flat the tree was standing in the bay window in the living room, as steady as though it still had its roots deep under the snow. Min smiled at it. It seemed to be basking in their approval, stretching out its branches in the warmth, bestowing upon them its spicy fragrance, displaying its soft needles for Maude to admire. She reached a slim paw to bat a springing bough.

"Hearken to me, Miss Motley," Jess said sternly. "This is not a cat's climbing frame. Or a trampoline."

Maude glanced at her, twitched her tail and stalked away with her nose in the air as though she were deeply affronted by the very suggestion that she would revert to kitten tricks. Jess covered her face with both hands and they all laughed.

"I'll fetch a few more decorations to keep you busy before I go," Jess said. She disappeared down the basement stairs.

Min and Toby did not speak to each other as he went

to work. The tree had been steadied even more in case of a possible pouncing cat when Jess came back with a stack of boxes holding lights and icicles and some homemade things – fat little angels shaped out of dough and painted in pastel colors. There were also origami birds and frogs and tiny colored boxes.

Min had never seen anything like them. She leaned over the array, her eyes shining. For a few blessed moments she completely forgot the small injured stray at the veterinary clinic. She almost forgot the boy.

"This blown glass ball hung on my adopted grandmother's tree years ago. She gave it to me on my first Christmas with them when I was seven," Jess said. "It's all greenish blue with no sparkly bits, but it seems far more magical to me than those others. Oh, and here's the star for the top. Toby, you climb up on the stepstool and I'll hand it up to you."

While Toby climbed the stepstool, Min took the blown glass ball and cradled it in her palm, trying to imagine it rounding out from the end of a glassblower's pipe. She had seen a program on different arts at school and had been entranced by the vases and flagons that took shape so beautifully. *Magical* was the right word.

Toby got the star fixed to the pointed twig at the very top and, as he began to come down, Jess said casually, "I was talking to your mother, by the way. You can spend the night if you like. The front bedroom is Min's, but the attic is still all yours."

Toby shot his godmother a look. Min knew it held some special meaning, but she could not tell what.

"Cool," he said, pulling out a box of glass icicles. "We'll have this job all done by the time you get back. No school tomorrow, of course, so I'm free. I said I'd ride herd on the Dittos tomorrow, though, while Mum shops, and on Christmas Eve too while she packs their stuff. You can imagine what it's like trying to do those things with Grace and Maggot pestering her."

"Just because her sister calls her Maggot doesn't mean you should," Jess told him, trying not to grin.

"But it suits her," Toby said.

"Do you know what a maggot is?" Jess asked.

"Okay, okay," Toby said. "The airport shuttle is picking us all up after supper on Christmas Eve. Mum has promised to take their Christmas stockings along so they can open them on the plane. Grace almost asked how Santa would get up there, but thought better of it. Sometimes the kid actually thinks."

Jess was shrugging into her coat while she listened. She smiled at the mental picture of the little girls with their stockings. "The airport shuttle will drop you here afterwards then?"

"That's the plan. Would you like me to try coming down the chimney?"

"Why not?" Jess said. "I think I have it clear now – maybe. You're staying here tonight, am I correct? I did ask Laura."

"Yup," Toby said, hanging another origami ornament on a pine branch.

Jess headed for the door. "Since I wasn't planning to go out to the veterinary clinic on the way home this afternoon, I have to get some milk and bread and stuff before we eat. I'll drop by and pick up the pizza on my way back. But I promise to return with maximum speed."

"Just remember poor Min is starving," Toby called after her. "Don't dawdle."

"I won't," she called back.

Once she was gone, Min stood stock still, staring into space.

Toby studied her. "What's eating you?" he asked roughly. "You look like you just lost your best friend. I'd say myself that you lucked out, landing here in time for Christmas."

"I don't have any best friend to lose," Min shot back. "I was just thinking about the dog Jess and I found today, that's all."

Toby swung around. "Dog? I wondered why she'd gone to the vet. I was afraid to ask in case something was wrong with Maude. What dog?"

When Min did not answer at once, he went on excitedly. "I love dogs, but my parents won't let me have one. My stepfather says he's allergic. I think it's a load of bull."

Min ignored the bad language and, after another moment's hesitation, plunged into the story of the little dog she and Jess had found in the ruined shed. Words poured out of her. She needed to talk about it. She wanted Toby to promise her the dog would live, would get all better. She told him everything, how it had cowered in the corner, how she had been afraid it was a rabid rat or squirrel.

"What kind of dog do you think it is?" he asked.

"The vet thought she might be a Peke," Min said, "but I've read books about them and this one didn't look like the pictures I've seen."

"Wait a sec. Jess has a really good dog book," Toby said, rushing to one corner of the room where there was a bookcase containing a couple of dozen reference books. "It'll be here. She has more than one about birds, one on trees, one about wildflowers, even one on bugs – all kinds of them. Here it is." He pulled a fat volume off the shelf and then added another thinner one.

Min forgot how nervous boys made her and leaned close, peering over his shoulder at the photos. He flipped through the pages, taking time to smile at certain pictures. She could tell he had been through the book lots of times. She would have herself if she'd been anyplace where such a book sat waiting.

"I love this book," he said. "It tells you what's good about every breed and warns you about which ones might bite kids or have back problems. The Net is good for researching any one breed, but this gives you the whole picture. Oh, here they are. Pekingese. Was she anything like this?"

Min felt her eyes sting as she stared at the fluffy, beautifully groomed dogs in the photographs. There were several colors and they were gorgeous. Their tails curled up proudly. Their coats shone with combing and brushing. Their ears hung down and yet seemed perky, and their black faces and button noses were adorable.

Not one of them looked like the throwaway dog in the shed, the quivering, ragged, filthy creature who had lain so still on the examining table.

Min could not speak. She pulled back and turned her head away.

Toby glanced at her to see why she was not answering. Then he closed the book. "She was in a bad way, you said. Don't compare her coat to these. Would she be about this size if she was healthy?" he asked, his voice quiet. "Was her nose black and did her eyes pop out a bit? Was she fluffy at all? I mean, will she be when she's clean or does she have short hair like a pug?"

Min turned back for another look. He had kept his finger in the place and he opened to it at once. Reluctantly, Min conjured up the picture of the wounded dog. "Her nose was jet black and her eyes did sort of pop a bit like those," she got out, in a shaking voice. "She was so dirty and so hurt, I couldn't tell much. She was creamy-beige maybe. And her bones stuck out. But she had hair … "

He pointed to another picture. "Maybe she's a Tibetan Spaniel? They look kind of the same. Champagne, they call this color."

"That's crazy," Min said, recovering her composure. "Champagne is like ginger ale, clear and bubbly."

"Maybe when she's clean she'll look totally different," he suggested. "I'll come to the vet's office with you tomorrow. I want to see her for myself."

Min jerked upright. Who did he think he was anyway? How dare he just push in like that!

"You can't!" she cried. Then, turning her back on him, she rushed out of the room. She fetched up in the kitchen and leaned on the counter, collecting herself. Then she got a glass of water. She stood still and drank half of it before she started back. He must have heard it running. She carried it back with her as an excuse for taking off so abruptly, although one look at his face told her he was not fooled for a minute.

"Jess'll let me come," he flung at her. "You wait and see. She isn't your mother, you know. Where is your mother, anyway? I think you have your nerve moving in on Jess right at Christmas."

Furious and frightened both, she gulped down the rest of the water while she scrabbled around, searching for a reply that would flatten him. "Well, I didn't ask you and, anyway, it's none of your business," she got out finally. "It was Jess's idea to bring me here, not mine. I haven't got a mother, if you must know, or a father or sisters either. So shut up."

Toby's mouth opened and closed and his eyes dropped. Her outburst had really shocked him and she was glad.

"Sorry," he mumbled. "What … what happened to your family?"

"I don't know and I don't care," Min yelled, amazed at

herself. "I thought you were going to have all those things hung on the tree before Jess comes back. Hadn't you better get going?"

Toby let the dog book slide off his lap and sprang to finish the job. The back of his neck looked very red.

She took a deep breath and went to help. They worked together, without speaking. Min had to concentrate because her fingers felt all thumbs. But slowly the rage drained away, leaving her feeling empty and cold inside.

"Pizza time!" Jess called, coming in bearing the familiar big boxes – two of them! "Tobe, run and get the other stuff from the van."

He was gone and back in seconds. The rich aroma of gooey cheese and spicy sausage reached their noses, and puppy mills were forgotten as they fell upon the food like hungry wolves. They were just getting well into their second slice when the telephone rang.

"You get it, Min," Jess groaned. "I'm too hungry to go. Maybe it's somebody trying to sell me something. Just say no!"

Min did her best to look totally calm as she went to pick up the receiver. She kept her back turned to the other two. "Dr. Hart's residence," she said.

"Min?" Sybil Willis exclaimed. "Heavens, you sound like a receptionist. Is Dr. Hart there?"

"She is," Min said, glancing over her shoulder at Jess, now collapsed in the largest easy chair. "But she's filling her face with pizza. I'll take the phone over to her, though."

As she crossed the room and held the receiver out to Jess, she grinned in spite of herself. Mrs. Willis must have been stunned. Min had always made a point of saying as few words as she could get away with, even when she had to talk to her caseworker. She did not know what had made her babble this time.

"Of *course* that was Min," Jess was saying. "She and I cut a Christmas tree down this afternoon and now she and Toby and I are taking a rest from trimming it. But if you want some pizza, you'll have to be quick to get any before Toby chomps down the last bite. Min has put away her share too, I hasten to add."

Sybil Willis did not accept the invitation. She began asking questions instead.

She never seemed nosy before, Min thought, while her insides knotted up and her hunger died.

"Of course she'll be with me until after Christmas," Jess snapped, straightening in the chair. "I told you that this morning. I hope she'll be with me much longer than that. I was needing a house elf."

Toby snickered. Min scowled but, inside, she was laughing too. She vowed she'd do a better job than Dobby or Kreacher in the Harry Potter books. She liked Dobby, in spite of his goofy ideas, but she was no house elf. She always wore matching socks, for one thing.

There was a silence. They could hear Mrs. Willis raving on. She sounded pretty upset, even though the kids could not catch her individual words.

"You know who Toby is, Syb. You've just forgotten. How old is he? What do you care? He's a little older than Min, but not much. You're twelve, aren't you, Tobe?"

Toby grinned and nodded.

"You do know him, Sybil – Laura's boy. You knew him when he was a baby."

As she talked, Toby slid out of his chair and stretched his long body out across the carpet. Then he crossed his eyes and stuck out his tongue. Min snorted with laughter, despite herself. Jess's eyes were sparkling but she only said, "Is there anything else you wanted to know, Sybil, or can I get on with my supper?"

They all heard Sybil bang down her receiver.

"She's nice," Min squeaked. "What did she want?"

"She has talked some more to that couple and they think they might even be interested in considering adoption later on, if you hit it off. She suggests I am being selfish. She does not want you hurt, that's for certain. She's a brick."

"A what?" Min asked, trying to picture her caseworker as a brick, trying not to hear the word *adoption*.

"My mother's mother used to say that," Jess said, grinning. "It means the same thing as 'She's a good egg.' Or 'She's a humdinger.' How about 'Right as a trivet,' 'She's a peach,' or 'She takes the cake?'"

Toby snorted but Min held onto her self-control and nodded, blushing faintly. She felt ashamed of laughing at Mrs.

Willis, who had been so good to her for so long.

"She really is pretty cool. She's the one who looked after me first," she muttered, remembering the shoes Mrs. Willis had kept for her. "She's … kind."

"I'm fond of her too," Jess said. "We've been friends for years, but I can't resist teasing her a little. She takes herself too seriously. She's done it since we were young."

"Hey, Rapunzel, help me clear up this mess," Toby said, putting on a saintly look and beginning to gather the garbage.

"What did you call me?" Min stuttered.

"Calm yourself, Rap. I haven't asked you to let down your rope of hair and haul me up to your tower window, have I?" He was smirking.

Min's eyes shot daggers at him. What was he talking about now? "Good thing," she growled.

Then she stalked out with Maude walking along behind her like a calico shadow. On the way, she realized she had heard of this dumb Rapunzel girl. She was the one whose hair was half a mile long and she made a ladder out of it – something like that. She put her hand up and gave her braid a gentle pat, but dropped it before anyone saw.

When they came back, Jess told them to follow her and led the way to the front door. Min reached for her coat, but Jess said not to bother. "We'll just be a minute."

"What the heck … ?" Toby drawled, trailing after them, trying to sound like a bored teenager.

Then they were in front of the house and Jess turned them

to look. In the bay window, the Christmas tree glowed like something out of a fairy tale.

"Oh …" Min breathed.

"Awesome," Toby said, laughing a little. "No, Jess. Don't hit me. I mean it."

"I think so myself," Jess said, shivering as the wind wrapped its chill arms around her. "Okay. Let's go back in."

Then Jess suggested a game of three-handed cribbage, but she yawned as she said it. Min had never played cribbage. She had never been placed with a game-playing family, so she was relieved Jess was sleepy.

"I'm too tired," Toby told her. "And so are you. We have to get up early to go and see that dog."

He glanced from Min's shocked face to Jess's sleepy one and waited. Jess's eyes woke up and searched Min's.

"Is he coming along or shall we send him about his business?" she asked in a voice that left the decision with Min.

"I'm – "

"Hold on, Tobe. This is Min's affair."

Min shrugged, fighting down a surge of resentment. He so clearly really wanted to see the little dog – and she was the one who had told him the story. If she didn't want to include him, she should have shut up about it.

"I guess it's okay," she said, watching him with a sideways look and feeling pleased when, despite her surly tone, he sent her a grateful grin.

Jess smiled and then turned back to Min. "Have you

86

named your little dog?" she asked. "I bet you have."

Min had a name ready, but she wasn't sure what they would think of it. "Emily," she murmured at last.

Jess nodded slowly. "I like it," she said finally. "Three of my all-time heroines are named Emily. Maybe we should make it Lady Emily to help make her proud of herself."

"Lady Emily sounds perfect," Min said.

Full of pizza, she suddenly was pleased that Toby would be there to share her love for the poor, wounded animal. Emily needed all the support they could find for her.

"I'll decide about the name when I've met her," Toby announced grandly, sticking his nose in the air. Min shot him a dirty look. He had obviously forgotten to be humble and gone right back to being his pushy self.

"Can we go first thing, before I have to go look after the Dittos?"

"Sure, if you get to sleep right away. I plan to leave early."

In her room, Min was so elated suddenly that she was sure she was not going to be bothered by her bad dreams. No nightmare would be able to follow her into this good place. And, first thing in the morning, she was going to see Emily. She wondered who Jess's heroines were. She herself loved a poem by a woman called Emily Dickinson, one she had found in a poetry book in the school library.

I'm nobody! Who are you? Emily Dickinson had written.

Min had told herself that that poem should be called "Min Randall." What had the writer of that poem been like?

Different, she was sure. Shy maybe. Like Lady Emily perhaps. But Emily was not nobody, not any longer.

Min hopped onto her bed, sat cross-legged and chanted softly.

She's somebody! Who is she?

She is Lady Emily.

And she is going to belong to me!

Maude, who had followed her in, gave her a wide stare and stalked out again. Min giggled and got ready for bed. She wasn't worried. Maude would be back.

7

Visiting Emily

M IN WAS RIGHT about the nightmare. She woke to see the sun peering over the roof across the road. It took so long to come up, this close to the longest night of the year. It must be well after eight.

She remembered Emily a second later and scrambled into her clothes in less time than it took the sun to complete its rising.

"Good morning, Min," Jess called as she appeared in the kitchen. "Come and eat. We have to rush. I have things to catch up on after lunch. Here you are."

She put a bowl of cornflakes topped with milk and sliced bananas in front of Min.

"I'll do some shoveling," Toby said, banging out through the back door.

Min ignored him. She did not begin to eat. "Do you think Emily is … is …" she began, her voice shaking.

"I called Jack a few minutes ago to see how she was doing, and she's still in the land of the living," Jess said quietly. "They've cleaned her up and she's on intravenous. She has a couple of cracked ribs and a crushed paw. Also, you will not be surprised to learn that over half of her teeth are rotten and will have to be extracted when she's strong enough. He says she has been treated cruelly, and shamefully neglected. She only weighs six and a half pounds, Min. Jack says she ought to weigh twice that much."

Min gulped. Her eyes smarted but she blinked away the threatening tears. Inside her head, she heard Enid Bangs's voice saying, *I tell you, the girl never cries.* Well, good old Enid didn't know everything. Min swiped the back of her hand across her eyes, to be on the safe side, and picked up her spoon.

"Can we bring her home today?" she asked.

"Not until after Christmas," Jess told her.

Min began to gobble her breakfast, her body telling her she would need strengthening for what might lie ahead.

"That was quick work," Jess said, removing the empty bowl. "Let's go."

Toby was the first one in the car, but Min was not wasting a thought on him now. All the way to the animal clinic, she fought down dread. What if Emily had died? What if something she had done had made her injuries worse? Or even killed her?

Don't be dumb, she told herself sharply. I didn't do anything but hold her. I did just what Jess told me.

They pulled up and Toby slid out of the back and swung Jess's door open.

"Thank you, Tobias," she said, grinning at him and reaching up as though she were going to rumple his hair.

"Don't ..." he yelped, ducking.

But Jess put on an innocent face. "Don't what?" she asked.

"Call me Tobias," Toby bellowed. But he was laughing.

Min knew, at once, that this was an old joke, a family tease. Envy bit at her again as she watched them.

Then she forgot them entirely. It was time to go in and see Emily.

"Well, you'll notice a big change," Dr. Miller said, coming into the waiting room. "I knew it would be you. Nobody else would drop in so early today. Your poor little dog lived through the night and seems a bit better, but she's not out of the woods yet, I'm afraid. We had one unpleasant surprise I haven't told you about yet. We found a shotgun pellet embedded in her flank."

"You mean ... someone *shot* her?" Min gasped.

"Maybe they just saw something moving and fired off a shot. We can be grateful they didn't try again. They didn't look for her though, although she must have yelped. Come this way and see how she is."

As they walked through to the back room, they passed a huge lop-eared rabbit that wiggled its nose at them and a couple of very young kittens curled up together. Toby smiled at them, but Min had eyes only for a small, sad dog. Where was she?

"Here we go," Dr. Miller said, undoing one of the cages.

Min stared at the limp bundle lying absolutely still inside. Emily was facing away from them. All the burrs were gone and her raggedy coat was a different color. A soft, creamy white instead of a dingy beige. But the thistledown fur was all different lengths. Her black nose looked surprisingly black now. An intravenous tube was dripping something into her paw, but she seemed unaware of it. Sharp bones were visible through her skin. Her hip bones looked like handles. If she had been a toy, you could easily have picked her up by one of them. Seeing how hurt she was, Min felt sick.

"My stepfather would say, 'That isn't a dog; that's a mouse.' He always says stuff like that about little dogs," Toby said, but his voice cracked. "He's wrong, of course."

"Of course," Dr. Miller echoed. "I've heard that line many times. But the very same men can turn to mush when they get a pup of their own. I think this little one of yours, Min, is asleep."

"Go ahead and stroke her, child," Jess said softly. "Just be very gentle. Say her name."

"Hello, Emily," Min crooned, touching the tiny dog with the tips of her fingers. The fur was so soft it was unbelievable. Emily's head came up for a moment and her tail lifted and trembled ever so slightly before it collapsed again. "Hi, there."

"Min named her this morning, Jack. What's the

prognosis?" Jess asked. "I know she's had a bad time, but you seem to think she might make it."

"I wish I was sure. I hope she'll pull through. But she's terribly weak. She's lost a lot of blood and these kinds of injuries take their toll. We can't tell if she's hurt inside, but I suspect she is. We'll certainly do our best for her, but she may well have internal injuries we can't spot."

"Who knows how long she'd been in the shed where we found her," Jess said.

"Not too long or she'd have frozen. It's been pretty cold at night this week. If you can figure out where she came from, I'd like to know. They should be reported to the authorities."

"Yes," Min and Toby said in unison. They shot a swift glance at each other and then quickly looked away. "I don't see how we can," Jess said, catching the glance and speaking sternly. "We certainly aren't going out there to ask around. My friend Mabel spoke of a place not all that far away where guard dogs are raised and trained. The place also has puppies for sale. Apparently, two women breed the small dogs and the brother of one of them trains the big dogs – they're really vicious. At least, that's the gossip. But Mabel doesn't know exactly where this place is and her neighbors claim the man prowls around with a shotgun and has put up *No Trespassing* signs. Mabel is upset about the gun, but then, people do hunt out that way. Since we have no proof that Emily came from there, we're not going anywhere near the place. Did you kids hear me?"

93

They nodded, but did not meet her eyes.

"Good thinking, Jess. Come on out to the desk and we'll discuss her treatment," the veterinarian said.

They walked away. Min and Toby stayed staring at Emily. When the adults were out of sight, Emily raised her tired head again and licked Min's hand with a tongue soft as a rose petal. Her eyes did not focus on them, though, but gazed into the distance. Then she put her head down again.

"Can she see? She can't be blind, can she?" Min whispered.

"I don't think so. Just too sick to care," Toby said.

Emily's small head was resting on her paws again and her eyes were shut, but her tail quivered once more, as though she were trying to wag it, yet lacked the strength.

"There's not much wrong with your tail anyway," Min told her, choking over the words. Her chest ached with love and pity for the dog who, through no fault of her own, had already suffered so much.

Toby reached out and gently shut the door of the cage. "I'd like to shoot them," he said, under his breath.

Min stared at him. "Would you go with me later to that place in the country?" she whispered. "I want to know what they're doing. I bet that stuff about the shotgun is just talk. But if they're hurting other little animals … "

Toby's answer, when it came, sounded jagged, as though slivers of glass were stuck to each word. "I vote we find out," he growled. "If it's true, we can report them. It'll take some planning, but we can do it. Jess would want to know too.

She just doesn't want us to get hurt. But we'd be careful. We might even be able to find out what we need to know, without them seeing us," he said, keeping his voice down to a whisper. "I might be able to get us a ride with my cousin next week sometime. Her best friend lives out that way and Martha drives over to visit her all the time. She's at home for the holidays right now. I'll check it out."

Min felt breathless. She was astonished at how quickly he had gotten it all planned. Seeing poor Emily lying there must be what had done it. She nodded and hung back to let him go ahead of her. She looked back once at the tiny, too-quiet dog, and was shocked to find her eyes filling with tears again.

Was she, cold-hearted Min, becoming a Moaning Myrtle? Why now?

Was it maybe because nobody here would jeer at her? Was it their trust that made her feel like bawling? Even so, she scrubbed all traces of tears away with her knuckles, thankful Toby was facing away from her.

"We'll be back and we'll find out who hurt you, Em," she promised under her breath.

Then she followed the boy she had been so sure she would hate.

8

Trinkets and Treasures

"NO SCHOOL FOR ALMOST TWO WEEKS," Toby exulted, once they were on their way. "I need to go home soon to babysit. But could you drop me off at my cousin Martha's first? Her house is right on your way and I have to talk to her about something."

"Martha?" Jess sounded as though he had spoken in a foreign language.

"Yeah – you know, my cousin Martha," Toby said, clearly annoyed at himself for talking when he should have kept quiet.

Min bent her head so neither of them would see her grin.

"I know who Martha is, Tobias. I just never guessed I'd hear you say you wanted to call on her," Jess said, still sounding amazed. "I thought you and she were bosom enemies. Whenever Martha's name is mentioned, you make disgusting noises, as I recall."

"It's her *mother* who really gives me a royal pain," Toby said. Then he laughed. "And she's not *your* favorite person either, Jess, so butt out."

Jess sent a haughty look his way and then chuckled. "I'm not fond of Lois, it is true, but you are not supposed to have noticed." She glanced at Min. "Lois is his stepfather's sister, and she's rather like our friend Enid."

Min's eyes widened and then she burst out laughing.

Toby gave his godmother a suspicious glance. "Who's Enid?"

"Never you mind. There's Martha's house up ahead. Get ready to jump out."

Toby unfastened his seat belt and made a parting shot. "I don't have to adore Aunt Lois to want to tell Martha something," he said loftily. "I do have a private life. I'll call you when I get home, Min. So long, Jessie."

As they watched him loping away, Jess smiled at Min, clearly delighted that the two of them were becoming friends. "I told you he wasn't so bad," she remarked, starting to drive away.

Min opened her mouth to straighten out any crazy ideas Jess was getting about their becoming friends, but then let it go. She, Min Randall, had never had any real friends. She was almost positive Toby was not about to change that. But she did quite like him after the way he had been with Emily. Jess let it be and they reached home in a companionable silence.

"I have some errands to run, but I'll drop you at the house. I know full well that you can take care of yourself for a bit. But I won't be long. And here's my cell number in case you need me," Jess said, as they pulled to a stop. "Here's your very own house key, too, so you can let yourself in."

The key was threaded on a loop of cord that Min hung around her neck at once. She pushed it down inside her clothes and waved to Jess. Then she had to pull it out to unlock the front door. She tried to look offhand, in case Jess was watching, but she felt extremely foolish. As the door swung open and she stepped inside, though, she felt a glow of pride. She belonged here. Anyone looking at her would know that.

Then she was alone in the house, expecting a call from Toby. Min realized suddenly she had never before waited for the telephone to ring, knowing the call would be for her. She fought down the sweet warmth that spread through her like hot fudge sauce poured over ice cream.

"Meow!"

"Oh, I'm sorry, Maude," she said, shrugging out of her coat and stooping to greet the cat. Maude purred forgivingly.

Min wandered out to the kitchen and had a drink of milk while she thought over the morning. Toby was actually going to come with her! He wasn't really her friend. She had only just met him, after all. Yet it felt as though she had known him far longer than a day.

Tomorrow he'd be back with them too. All at once she realized she was looking forward to his coming. She reached for the picture of him with his family and smiled at his sulky expression. He didn't enjoy having his picture taken. Neither did she.

Hastily she replaced the photograph and backed away.

"I must be losing my grip," she muttered to Maude.

Yet he was planning to help her find out who had hurt Emily. Emily was the one he cared about, the one that mattered to both of them.

But I *still* do not trust boys, she decided.

She was starting on a list of all the rotten boys who had been with her in foster care and at school. Laird Bentham was the worst – the bully who had first taunted her with those awful nicknames. He and his one friend told everyone that she had been found in a dumpster.

She had tried, long ago, to set that straight. She had punched him in the face. Nobody had stuck up for her. Nobody had told the teacher that Min had not started the trouble or that she had only been defending herself.

"March yourself down to the office," Mrs. Short-Whitman had snapped at her. "You too, Laird."

She had gone to the office, head high, with Laird trailing along behind her, snickering. She had been ready to demand justice. But the vice-principal had been in no mood to listen.

"I presume you can explain this outrageous behavior, Minerva," he had rasped, glowering at her. He must have known Laird had begun it, but he had not let on.

How could she explain? She would have had to repeat Laird's taunts with him standing there with his hand pressed to his face. She had said nothing, but she had stared hard at his bloody nose and smiled very slightly, too fast for the man to catch, but making sure Laird got the threat in that smile. He had given a little squawk and Mr. Downing's eyes had bored into her like drill bits. She was expelled for three days because of the school's Zero Tolerance for Violence policy. Enid had, of course, phoned Mrs. Willis. When Mrs. Willis asked Min if it was something she should worry about, Min had told her to forget it. "I'll ignore him," she had promised.

But, even now, remembering Laird Bentham sauntering out of the office, smirking, while she had to go home and face Enid's sharp scolding, made her so mad she picked up a couch cushion and pitched it across the room. Too late, she saw Maude up on the back of the easy chair. The flying cushion missed the cat by miles, but she sprang up to the top of the cat tree and yowled in protest, her fur standing up like a bottle brush.

"Oh, Maude, I'm so sorry," Min cried, rushing over and lifting her into her arms and stroking her head. The cat slowly became once again a peaceful pet. The two of them settled down together into the chair next to the phone.

Then, out of the blue, it came to Min that moving in with Jess might mean that she would be changing schools. Maybe she would actually get a true fresh start, and not have to fear that the story of her being abandoned would follow her. Maybe she would shed it like a snake leaving its too-small, dusty old skin behind. She had seen such a skin once, empty and tattered, lying discarded and forgotten in the dirt.

She wondered idly if the snake felt the way kids must feel

when they were dressed all in new clothes from the skin out. She thought she remembered Robin Randall dressing her up like that. There had even been a hat with flowers. Had it been for Easter, maybe? Min was no longer sure.

Maude had begun to purr like a buzz saw. Min blew gently on one of her ears and watched it flick. The purring went on, louder if anything. It was making her sleepy.

Then, all at once, the phone rang. Min jumped like a startled rabbit, making the cat break off her purring abruptly. Then she reached for the phone with an unsteady hand. "Hello," she said, barely able to get the word out.

"What's the matter with you?" Toby demanded. He did not wait for her to answer, for which Min was grateful. "I've got a ride for us with my cousin. I told her we wanted to go tobogganing. You said there was a big hill. We have to wait until next week, but that's good, really. They'd notice if we took off so close to Christmas."

"Right," Min got out.

Talking on the phone was hard. Her throat kept squeezing the words until they were as thin as bits of thread. But he did not comment again.

"It's okay with you then?" he asked.

"Okay," Min said, feeling as if she were strangling.

"Hey, Min, you all right?"

"Sure. It's great. See you," she answered and hung up before he could ask her any more unanswerable questions.

Maude grunted and resettled herself with an annoyed

switch of her tail. She clearly did not approve of people giving their attention to the telephone, when she was right there on top of them.

"Sorry, puss," Min murmured.

The two of them curled up together in front of the TV and watched a DVD Jess had left there. It was a corny old Christmas movie. All the children were wide-eyed and incredibly sweet. People were slipping presents under the tree or busy wrapping gifts for Grandma. Older kids were out carol singing. Min glared at the screen and then froze.

Gifts!

She had totally forgotten gifts, and it was only two days until Christmas. Min knew, all at once, that Jess would give her presents. She did not know how she knew this, but she was suddenly positive. Maybe Toby would be made to do it too.

Could she … should she try to give something to them? What? In all her life, Min had never gone out and chosen a gift for someone and given it to the person. She had presented things that were given to her to give. "Here's perfume you can give Enid," Mrs. Willis had said. "I even had it gift-wrapped for you. But you have to sign the card."

How she had resented signing that card with a kitten sitting in a basket decked with holly. Ugh!

They'd made stuff for their parents at school and Min had always thrown the ugly, lumpy things away in the first garbage can she came to on the way home. The grubby cloth pencil case, the toothbrush holder made of popsicle sticks, the drooping bean plant in its tiny pot, the incredibly ugly ashtray poster-painted a ghastly purple.

This year she had already pitched the knobbly candy dish she had fashioned in Art class. She would have been embarrassed to give it to anyone. If she'd spent time and thought on it, it might have been okay, but she had poked the clammy clay into a lopsided saucer shape and pressed in the colored macaroni pieces around the edge as fast and furiously as she could. It was almost splendid in its ugliness.

"I can't understand how a girl who draws as well as you do can produce something this ugly, Min," the Art teacher had said, staring at the thing.

Min could have told her. She loved drawing, but she never took anything home. When what she made was supposed to be a gift or a Mother's Day card, she tried to do her worst rather than her best.

Min had shaken her head and silently put the hideous object with the rest to dry out. Hers was not the only ugly one, she noticed. But most were good enough to give to someone. Not hers though. Even Jess would not have been able to think of anything polite to say about it.

Yet she must have a present for Jess. Suddenly she longed desperately to come up with a splendid present, something special that would tell her how Min felt about her.

But what could it be? And if she thought of the perfect present, how would she pay for it? Even painting a picture to give would require paper and paints, and although Min loved to draw and paint, she could not manage it without supplies.

She went on sitting in front of the television, but no longer followed the story. She felt as though she'd swallowed a stone. Not just any stone. A great lump of grey granite with sharp edges. There was no way she could produce anything worth presenting.

When Jess came home, Min's head rested on the cushion she had thrown so furiously across the room an hour earlier and she was asleep. Jess pulled an afghan over her and switched off the TV.

Min did not wake until dishes clinked in the kitchen. She yawned and then went to help get lunch.

"Welcome, cook's assistant," Jess said as Min started to set the table without being told.

When they had finished, Jess yawned, in her turn, and said, "Wake me up in fifteen minutes. I have a lot to do before the holiday."

She went to the living room and sat in the big chair facing the Christmas tree. In two minutes she was asleep. Min had opened her mouth to ask how she would know. She had no watch. But Jess had fallen asleep as suddenly and completely as a felled tree. Min stared at her and wondered what she should do. Then she crept away and went through the house looking for clocks. There was one on the stove and there was also a timer on top. Min set the timer and watched the clock face. The cat stared at her, as if puzzled by her keeping this silent vigil.

"Time's up," Min said, gently, right on the dot. "I was wondering why you call Toby *Toby?* I heard his mum calling him Tobias."

"Laura does not believe in nicknames, but I do," Jess said. "If you could have seen how small he was, you would know that Tobias was too heavy a name for such a scrap. I could hold his whole little body in my cupped hands. His dad calls him Toby too, although Baxter always says Tobias."

Min filled their water glasses and sat down at her place. Then she asked, hesitantly, "Do you know where his ... his real father is right now?"

"Patrick? In Indonesia or Sri Lanka, last I heard. But he's supposed to be coming home to spend Toby's holidays with him," Jess answered.

They ate quickly. Min had gone back to trying to think of how to come up with gifts. She was startled when Jess pushed back her stool and spoke to the cat. "Maudie, take care of Min. I have Christmas shopping to do, among other things. I got you a warm hat this morning, by the way, Min. It's with your coat in the back hall. Oh, here's some Christmas money for you and a wallet to keep it in until you spend it. You can walk downtown from here if you like or I can drive you later on. Do you know the way?"

Min nodded dumbly, her eyes huge.

Jess smiled at her. "Fine. See you later. I'll be back well

before supper."

She was gone. Min sat frozen in her chair until Maude Motley butted her ankle with her bullet head.

"Oh, Maudie, how did she guess?" the girl asked the cat, leaning down to stroke her. Maude paced down the hall to the front room with its enticing tree. Then she purred and curled up in Jess's chair, nose tucked under her tail. Min perched on the couch and examined the wallet. Then she counted the money with hands that trembled. Fifty dollars! She had never had money she was free to spend in any way she pleased, never in her life. She sat staring at it, dumbfounded by the knowledge of its buying power and by the feel of it in her fingers. She unzipped the change pocket and found two toonies and a loonie. Another five dollars!

And she had not even thanked Jess!

She leaped up and raced to the back door and, as the car backed down the driveway, she waved the wallet and called, "Thank you, Dr. Hart!"

The car stopped. Jess's head poked out.

"Who is Dr. Hart?" she asked, laughing. "I don't think she lives around here."

Min got the giggles. They bubbled up in her and could not be squashed enough for her voice to come out clearly.

"Thanks, Jess," she burbled, tears in her eyes and her cheeks burning with embarrassment and delight.

"You are entirely welcome," Jess answered and drove away with a swoosh.

Min found the hat Jess had bought for her. It was bright red. She pulled it on, added coat and mitts and set out for downtown. She was about to try her hand at Christmas shopping. She wandered up Quebec Street, peering into every store she passed. She had been inside a couple of stores on the main street but had found nothing inexpensive and yet special. She had made herself a Christmas list. Jess of course, Mrs. Willis, Maude Motley … ?, Toby, maybe, and Emily. Five presents to buy. She went into The Bookshelf first and saw a paperback dog book Toby would like if he didn't have it already. She looked inside. It had just been published. She paid for it with trembling hands and left before she could be tempted to buy something for herself.

What next?

She saw a sign reading *TRINKETS AND TREASURES* and her spirits rose like singing larks. It sounded like the very place she needed. Trinkets, after all, were small and should not cost too much. Feeling shy suddenly, she opened the door carefully and eased her body through the crack.

"Hi there," the woman inside said. "Where did you spring from?"

Min wanted to back out again until she saw the warmth in the woman's smiling eyes.

"I'm Raymah," she was saying. "You know what? I'll bet I know you."

Min began to shake her head when Raymah said, "You're Min. I forget your other name. Jess Hart was telling me

107

about you and how excited she is that you'll be with her this Christmas. Also, the hat you are wearing came from this very store. She said she'd send you here."

Jess must have forgotten, Min thought, but she smiled back at last. "Yes. I'm Min. And I want to get Jess a present," she confided.

"Well, I can show you the things she picks up and holds and then puts down," Raymah said. "These beeswax candles, to start with. And this Christmas tree decoration." She was holding up a tiny pair of carved wooden shoes.

Min looked at the things. Then, on the counter, she saw a ceramic dog dish. On the side it said *YUM!*

"How much is this?" she asked, touching it with one mittened hand.

"Eight dollars," Raymah told her. "A friend makes them for me. But Jess doesn't have a dog, does she?"

Next thing Min knew, she was pouring out the story of finding Emily and bringing her home. She was amazed at how easy it was to tell this Raymah all about the rescue, as though she, Min, had always been a chatterbox.

"For Emily, I'll sell it to you for five," Raymah said, putting the bowl into a bag. "How about a catnip mouse for Maude? You don't want to hurt her feelings."

"No," Min said, taking it from her. Then she found a little carved wooden angel with outstretched arms that she decided to give to Mrs. Willis. She spent all her money in Raymah's shop except for the coins, and was on her way out when she caught sight of a pad of drawing paper with a box of pencil crayons propped invitingly beside it. She hesitated. Then she went back and asked Raymah how much they cost.

"How much have you got left?" Raymah asked, her eyes sparkling.

Min told her.

"This is your lucky day," the woman said, putting the drawing things into a paper bag. "But it will cost you your last penny."

Min was pretty sure Raymah was not telling her the full price, but she could not bring herself to protest. She took the bag, added it to the rest of her things and gave the woman a smile very few people had ever glimpsed. "Thank you," she said softly.

"Merry Christmas, Min," Raymah said, smiling back.

Min put the things she had purchased carefully into the tote bag she had bought earlier. She felt herself smiling with immense satisfaction. Each thing she had bought was a treasure, not a mere trinket. Her tote said *Reading Matters* on it. Min thought reading did matter. She was halfway through *Chance and the Butterfly*. Her heart ached for Chance even though he was much younger than she was.

When she got home, the winter dark was drawing in, making the bare trees a bit frightening as they rattled their stripped branches in the strengthening wind. Her red hat kept her ears warm as toast, but her nose felt raw and her cheeks stung. The door was locked so she used her key, feeling proud all over again. Yet when she got inside, she was foolishly disappointed to find no Jess waiting to welcome her.

Then the phone rang. She hesitated, sure it would not be for her, but picked it up just as Jess's answering machine clicked on. She was hanging up when she heard the veterinarian's voice sounding troubled. She stiffened and listened.

"Jess," he said, "It's Jack. I thought I should warn you. The little Peke nearly died this afternoon. We kept her heart beating, but she may well die before you bring the kids out here after Christmas. I thought you should be prepared. She's alive now but very weak. She's had a rough – "

The machine cut him off before he had finished his sentence. Min hung up the receiver and undid her coat with numb fingers. Should she tell Jess? She didn't think she could. She went into her room and lay face down on the bed, weeping into her pillow.

When Jess came home, she found Min asleep for the second time that day. She was about to wake her so that she would not have trouble falling asleep later, when she noticed the pile of soggy Kleenex next to her hand. Leaving her be, she greeted Maude and checked for telephone messages.

After listening to Jack's worried voice reporting on Emily, she understood. She went into the living room and, letting the cat settle in her lap, sat and thought deeply. Christmas was the day after tomorrow. It would be Min's first real one. A day of festivity and celebration to make up for all the miserable Christmases that Min had endured before, was what Jess had planned. But how could they celebrate if Emily was to die on Christmas Eve?

The telephone interrupted her reverie. "Hold on, Laura. I'll take the call in my study," she murmured.

The phone's ringing woke Min. She sat up and tried to look as if she were feeling fine.

Jess hung up, came to her door and smiled at her. "I thought I was finished shopping, but I have one more errand to run later. How did you get along?"

The look of dull misery dropped from Min's face like a discarded Halloween mask. Her dark eyes shone with excitement. "I have something for everyone, even Mrs. Willis," she said. "I can't show you yours, of course, but would you like to see what I found for Toby and Maude and Mrs. Willis … and Emily."

"Show me," Jess said. "I can hardly wait."

Leaving the drawing things hidden, Min pulled out the dog bowl without a word and, setting it aside, displayed first the catnip mouse and then the paperback dog book she had found for Toby. Last, she produced the wooden angel.

"Perfect, Min," Jess said. She batted Maude Motley's nose away from the bag containing her mouse. "Not yet, cat. Have you no sense of occasion?"

After displaying each present ceremoniously, Min hid

them all away in her dresser drawer.

"Come and eat," Jess said as she returned. "I brought some fast food home with me. Let's take it and eat in front of the fireplace. This is the sort of day that needs rounding out with a fire."

Min opened her mouth to mention the call from the veterinarian and then took a bite of hamburger instead. She did not want to cry in front of Jess. If she did, she might be unable to keep herself strong and all in one piece. If she kept bursting into tears she would lose control. She felt, without knowing why, that if she lost control, she might lose her self somehow and never be able to find it again.

Maude jumped up and butted her head against the edge of Min's empty plate.

"Hope springs eternal in that creature," Jess said. "Harden your heart, Min. Push her off."

Min showed Maude the empty plate and apologized instead. The cat gave her a sorrowful glance and dropped to the floor with a thud.

After supper, Jess disappeared into her study. Min caught the murmur of her voice talking to someone on the phone. "Oh, I was sure I would be too late. You are wonderful," she heard. "I know I'm crazy, but so are you. I'll be there in an hour. Don't let anyone else have her. Yes, I know I want her sight unseen."

Her? Who was this *her?*

Min felt distinctly uneasy as she turned the word over in

her mind. What on earth was Jess up to now? Not another foster daughter! That would be unthinkable. She already had to share Jess with a godson.

The person thought Jess was crazy, though. That might refer to another needy kid's moving in. She trailed after Jess from the moment she reappeared, hoping for a reassuring explanation, but none came. She did seem to be grinning but, after all, Christmas was practically here.

"I have one last errand to run," Jess said when the hour was almost up. "But I'll be right back."

"Would you like me to come with you?" Min asked, doing her best to sound casual, staring at the hall carpet.

"Not this time, but thanks for offering. Get your pajamas on and we can watch the new Christmas DVD I picked up this afternoon."

While Jess was away, Min got out the paper and drawing pencils. She sat on her bed, knees drawn up, with the light shining down on what she was drawing, and concentrated on making a picture she had dreamed up on her walk home. She made two false starts and almost gave up in despair. Then, suddenly, her hand seemed to catch on to what she wanted and the idea began to flower on her page. She smiled. If only it came out right, she knew Jess would like having it.

Jess was back in an hour. Min moved like lightning to hide her picture. It needed a few finishing touches, but otherwise it was fine. Then she sped out to inspect whatever Jess had gone to get. But Jess's hands were empty. No mysterious bundles. It was very strange. No "her." Min heaved a sigh, half impatience, half relief.

"Let's leave the movie and go to bed instead," Jess said, catching Min stifling a yawn. "I am reading a great book. Tomorrow night will be Christmas Eve, you know, and there won't be time to spare – not even for Barbara Kingsolver."

"What's it called?" Min asked idly.

Jess laughed. "*Pigs in Heaven*," she said. "It's about a young woman who finds a baby and ends up adopting her. Well, it's the second book about her. Good night. Sleep well, daughter."

Min turned out her light obediently and waited until she was sure Jess was safely settled in her own room. Then she tiptoed to her dresser and eased out her picture. It was still good. Pushing away Maude's inquisitive nose, she went back to work and spent great care adding the final touches. When it was as good as she could make it, she hid it again and went to bed to think once more about the mysterious "her" who was coming. But she couldn't work up any real worry, not while she had her picture to think about. Soon she drifted off despite her excitement. And, even though a nightmare did hover on the edge of her slumber, a huge calico cat, the size of a lion but called Sugarplum, fought off the threatening darkness and purred her into a peaceful sleep.

9

The Mysterious "Her"

THE NEXT MORNING, Sybil Willis came over with a box of Christmas cookies she had baked for them. They were wonderful, all different shapes, iced – and yummy.

After they had sampled some, Min presented Mrs. Willis with a box containing the carving of the small wooden angel with her arms out, flying for all she was worth. She had wrapped the box with great care and written on a card, *This is what you are to unhappy children.*

Jess, when shown the card earlier, had given Min a quizzical look. "It would delight her if you added *especially me* to the message," she said gently. "And it would be true, wouldn't it? Sybil has been standing up for you ever since I've known the two of you."

"I guess," Min said grudgingly. She had thought the card was fine, and it wasn't Jess's business.

"Sorry," Jess said. "It is a perfect gift and a lovely message. Sometime I may learn when to keep my mouth shut."

Min had kept her back turned and placed the package at the base of the Christmas tree. She felt something hard inside her balk at her own sudden wish to agree and say she would add Jess's words. Why should she? The angel was from her, not Jess. And she had been so pleased with what she had written. She clamped her lips together and did not answer.

But later on, when Jess was not watching, she had gone back and added the two words, knowing they were exactly right.

When Mrs. Willis saw the angel, she smiled. When she read the message, her eyes filled with tears that she hastily brushed away. She held out the card for Jess to read and Jess's eyes met Min's in a wordless smile. Not noticing, Sybil Willis went on. "I know what you think of people who weep, Min. Wimps. But sometimes it can't be helped."

Thrown off balance, Min had no answer ready and just let her smile grow to take in both women.

Parcels had been arriving at the door and in the mail even on the day before Christmas. Most were for Jess, of course, but at least four were for Min – one from Jess, one from Maude, one from Toby and later, another one from Jess. Min was eaten up with curiosity. She could not remember being given anything before that was not dull and totally sensible. They had never been meaningful things chosen especially with her in mind. These were bound to be different. She shook the parcels gently and squeezed them and even held them up to her nose. But she could not be sure of any of the contents, and Christmas morning still seemed years away.

"It's Christmas Eve tonight," she reminded herself – but it still sounded as though it would stretch out forever.

When Christmas Eve itself finally did arrive, Jess showed her a large felt Christmas stocking decorated with snowflakes and with Min's name written with fabric paint at the top. She hung it in front of the fireplace with her own and Maude's and one for Toby.

"Oh, I haven't filled you in," Jess said suddenly. "Laura phoned. Toby's father couldn't get a flight until the day after Boxing Day, and as I said, Laura's leaving tonight with the twins. Toby's going to the airport with them to help Laura get safely as far as Security with the girls and the luggage. Then, when they're gone, he'll get dropped off here late tonight. He has a key, of course, so he'll let himself in and go right up to bed without waking us. That's the plan, anyway."

"I wonder if the twins are excited," Min said, calling their small, eager faces to mind. Too bad Toby wasn't going with his mother and leaving Maggot and Grace behind. It would be fun celebrating Christmas with two such comical, lively children.

"So Toby will be staying with us a bit longer than he thought," Jess went on. "He'll go off with Patrick when he finally arrives. Patrick doesn't always get things arranged far enough ahead of time. Baxter, on the other hand, invariably has every detail organized. He must be a bit daunted by all this changing, but it is his mother's doing, not his wife's."

"Oh," Min said, half listening.

Her stomach felt strange. She was not sure why. But she knew it was mostly compounded of pleasure and panic. How would she and Toby hit it off stuck in the same house for days? Would he still mind her horning in? She stared at the stockings hung by the fireplace with care and hoped she would know what to do when the time came.

She woke once, just after midnight, and went to her window to gaze up at the starry sky. Words, which had not registered in her mind before, sang in her head now. It really was "a midnight clear." An icy draft chilled her bare feet and she jumped back into her warm bed and curled herself up into a cocoon of sleep. She woke once again, but stayed in bed, her eyes firmly shut, not wanting to wake up properly until morning.

It seemed only a moment later that she heard Jess's voice singing, "O come, all ye faithful." Min kept her eyes shut and exulted in the knowledge that Christmas had dawned at last.

Then a soft, wiggling weight plumped down onto her chest and she opened her eyes to see the small, jet-black face of a Pekingese puppy staring down at her.

Min stared back, convinced she was dreaming. It couldn't

be real. Then the puppy licked her nose. The soft, wet tongue was very real indeed.

"Who … ? What … ?" Min stammered, shrugging free of her covers so she could reach out and hold onto the warm bundle. "Who … ?"

She couldn't be dreaming. But she couldn't understand any of it either.

The puppy leaned down and gave Min's chin a quick lick. Then it shook its head briskly so that its ears flew out to either side.

Jess was laughing too hard to speak. Or perhaps crying. Her eyes were suspiciously wet.

"Who … ?" Min squeaked again, cradling the small, warm puppy in both hands and sitting bolt upright so she could get a closer look and a better grip.

"Merry Christmas, Min. I don't know who she is. They've been calling her Jill, but you'll have to christen her properly. I don't think *Jill* fits. She's eight weeks old and she weighs two pounds. She's a brindle Peke with a blond tail. If she doesn't grow much bigger, she'll be a sleeve dog. I think she is adorable, myself. But she's not mine, she's yours."

"Oh, Jess … she's … she's the most beautiful –"

The puppy bounced up and batted Min on the chin with her tiny paw, not letting her finish. Min caught the foot in her fingers. It felt so soft, as though it were made of yarn instead of muscle and bone. Afraid of hurting her, Min let go instantly.

"Come on, both of you. She wants to see what's in her stocking."

"Did Toby come?" Min asked.

"Yes, but he didn't arrive until almost midnight. I was afraid your puppy would wake up, so I didn't get up to say hello. I wanted you to see her first."

Min could not think how to tell her how grateful she was that she had met her puppy before Toby laid eyes on her. She kissed the top of the pup's head and sent a look of intense happiness at Jess.

Jess grinned back and gave her braid a gentle tug. "I'll bet the boy joins us in no time. He hasn't reached the stodgy adult stage of wanting to sleep late on Christmas morning," she said.

Min had scrambled out of bed. She now put her slippers and dressing gown on without once letting go of her incredible wiggly present. She did not believe in the puppy yet, but snuggling her close, she tipped the small face up to her cheek with one finger and murmured love words as she trailed Jess across the hall.

"Put her down quietly and let Maude look her over. I kept the puppy shut up all night in the little room off the kitchen, and Maude Motley has been driven mad by the puppy noises and smells," Jess said.

Min sank to the floor and put the tiny dog down on the carpet. Maude hissed and her tail stuck straight up like an exclamation point.

Mopsy … Button … Sweetie … Min thought dazedly, as she watched the two stare at each other.

"She surely *is* a sweet, wee lassie," Jess crooned.

"Cassie," Min said, knowing, all at once, what the puppy's name was. "Her name is Cassie. But, Jess, is Emily … Emily didn't … Has she … ?"

She could not finish the question. What if Jess had bought Cassie because she'd heard that Emily had died in the night?

"Emily is still alive. I called before I woke you," Jess said quietly. "If she grows strong enough, she'll come home to us and Cassie can teach her how to be a normal little dog. Jack thinks Emily has never had a chance at a normal life. He also thinks she may be a Tibetan Spaniel rather than a Peke. But don't worry about robbing Emily of love by loving Cassie, Min. Your heart holds more than enough love for two small dogs – love I believe you've had scant chance to spend. Look. Here's her Christmas stocking and here's yours."

"How about mine?" Toby asked from the doorway in a voice blurred with sleep.

"I was about to call you. You must be half dead, but I was sure you would not want to miss anything," Jess said.

"When did you come in?" Min asked. Then, before he could answer, she held up her puppy. "Look!" she cried. "Isn't she perfect?"

Toby blinked. Staring at the tiny, wiggling mop in Min's arms, he asked, "What is it? A new kind of feather duster?"

Then, as Min prepared to blast him, he gave way to an

enormous smile and extended his hand open for sniffing to the nose in the small black face.

"She's my present – and she's no duster. Cassie is my Pekingese," Min said, pretending to be huffy but really bursting with pride.

Maude gave such an outraged meow that Min went straight to the piano bench and fetched the catnip mouse she had hidden there before she went to bed.

"Okay, Queen Maude, here's a gift for you," she said, stooping to toss it to the cat.

Maude turned her back on the puppy and leaped onto the toy as joyously as a kitten. She tossed it in the air, caught it, jumped on it and rubbed her face against it. Cassie watched her with her round eyes practically popping out.

By this time Toby had collected his stocking. He sat on the floor to investigate its contents. Despite her curiosity about hers, Min was almost too entranced by Cassie to dig into the heap of small presents that bulged within it, stuffing it to the top.

Finally Jess reached out, captured the puppy and lifted her onto her lap.

"Start on that stocking before I give it all away to some other girl," she said. "I have never filled a stocking for you before and I want to see if I did a good job."

"You mean Santa didn't fill it?" Min teased, trying to look shocked. "I always thought –"

"Min, do you want me to expire before your very eyes? I

am one of his helpers, you dolt."

At last, Min began to discover what Santa Claus, a.k.a. Jess, had brought her. There was a package of pens in assorted colors, a marzipan pig, a beanbag shaped like an owl, a book that told her fortune for every day in the coming year, a pad of Post-it Notes, a tube of striped toothpaste, a box of Macintosh's Toffee, a chocolate letter *M*, a mandarin orange and a toonie. In the toe was a small, fancy box containing a digital wristwatch.

Min had never owned a watch. She gaped at it and drew in her breath sharply. Toby glanced over and whistled.

"Cool," he said and began to peel his orange.

"I was dimly aware of you searching the house for clocks the other day," Jess said, grinning. "Finally I realized why. Now, you two, let's leave the rest until after breakfast."

"No. I want you two to have your presents from me," Min said. She felt her face flushing with uncertainty and excitement. After all, she had never done this before. But she left Cassie on Jess's knee while she dug out the presents she had wrapped for Jess and Toby. All the parcels looked small and insignificant now. With her heart beating fast, she presented them without a word, scooping Cassie out of Jess's arms so she would have both hands free. For the first time, she actually ignored the wriggly puppy while she watched.

Jess undid first the tiny, perfect carving of a chickadee and then the honey-scented candles. "Oh, Min, how did you guess?" she said, clearly delighted. She stroked the chickadee's tiny head with a fingertip and sniffed the honey-scented candles.

"Raymah told me what you'd like," Min mumbled.

"Well done, Raymah," Jess said. Then she stood up and came over to kiss Min's cheek. "Thank you so much, my sweet."

Min was horrified. She had loved the lapful of loot she had taken out of her stocking, but she had not remembered to thank Jess. She certainly had not kissed her!

"I'm sorry," she began, blushing scarlet. "I never said thank you … But I love the things."

"Don't be ridiculous. Your shining face thanked me for every trifle and your joy over Cassie was beautiful to behold."

Now Min's attention had shifted, though. She was watching Toby out of the corner of her eye. He ripped off the paper and began to leaf through the book's pages, exclaiming with delight at the pictures and the detailed history of each breed. He didn't say thank you either, but Min saw at once how much he loved it and realized Jess had been right about words not always being needed.

Jess peered down at the picture of a champion Pekingese he was looking at and smiled.

"Good choice," she said. "Now let's eat. The eggnog is poured and waffle batter is waiting."

Min could not bear to put Cassie down on the floor. Keeping her on her lap, she sipped her eggnog and then started in on her first bite of waffle.

"I can't believe this," Toby said, staring at Cassie's head, which had popped up to see what they were up to.

"Me neither," Min answered, smiling a smile he had never glimpsed before. His startled expression told her she had been transformed somehow and she ducked her head and hid her hot face behind Cassie's. When she raised it again, she was almost back to her usual self.

"She'll have to learn some table manners," Jess said firmly, pretending to glare at the puppy.

"Like what?" Toby asked through a mouthful of waffle.

"Dogs watch people at tables eat, but they stay on the floor while they watch and they get no handouts during meals. Today being Christmas, we'll pretend Min is not sneaking tidbits into the mouth of a greedy Peke pup."

They all laughed as Cassie gave a small yip of protest. Then, after they had cleared the table, Jess led the way back to the front room, got out the Bible and read the story of the first Christmas aloud. The old story made Min think of the homeless stone family downtown. She was glad the baby Jesus had been born in a warm stable instead of by the roadside.

The rest of the day went on being magical, even when Cassie tried to eat a piece of toffee and got her baby teeth thoroughly stuck, and when Maude Motley, wanting to be a part of things, ate the wishbone before they could pull it. Both pets survived, but not without drama.

Toby kept eyeing the telephone, sure his father would call. But the only long-distance ring was from his mother, saying

that they had arrived safely and that opening their stockings
on the airplane had been a great success.

That night, Cassie was put to bed in a snug box fitted up
for a small dog's bedroom, but Min and Toby and even Jess
knew perfectly well that she was going to spend most of the
night snuggled up with Min. They were all tired after the day.
They had worked on a gigantic jigsaw puzzle Toby had given
them both as a family present. They put on a CD of British
choirs singing carols. They had eaten enough turkey for four
or five people and had been almost too full for dessert.

"We can save it," Jess said. "Midnight snacks."

"I don't think I can make it to midnight," Toby said,
yawning widely. "But I want to download some music onto
my iPod."

The two of them consulted on which tunes he should
choose and Jess let them pay for them with her credit card.

Nobody turned on the television. Nobody switched on
the radio to listen to the news. It was as though the three
people, the cat and the puppy spent their first Christmas
together inside an enchanted bubble into which nothing
worrying could break.

When it was time to go to bed, Min finally got up
the courage to carry the drawing she had made into Jess's
bedroom. She had planned to prop it up against the pillows,
but Jess herself came in and caught her in the act. She took

the drawing and gazed at it, her eyes wide.

It was a picture of a Christmas tree under a starry sky. On its branches were the decorations they had used, but next to the felt and feather birds sat real ones – chickadees and a cardinal. At the foot, a blue jay strutted. There was also a baby fox scampering off with one of the balls and Maude Motley sitting up tall, gazing up at the star on the top. There was no pot to hold the trunk because the tree was clearly alive, but it looked as though it was celebrating Christmas from its unseen roots to the star on its tip. At the bottom, carefully lettered, were the words *A Tree for Jess*.

"Oh, Min, how … how wonderful," Jess whispered.

The hug that followed was nice but, when Min and Cassie were in bed, Min knew that the look on Jess's face and the hush with which she spoke were her most precious moments – next to her unbelievable introduction to her Cassie.

She lay there with the puppy – tired out at last – curled up next to her chin and started going over it all, the first truly merry Christmas she could remember. But she dozed off before she had finished gloating over even half the jewel-bright memories.

And no bad dreams came to shadow her joy.

10

Lost Fathers

THEY ALL SLEPT IN and had to rush to be ready for church.

Jess went to the old stone church that was right across from the bench on which Min had sat studying the statue of the happy family less than a week before. Glimpsing it when they got out of the van, Min found it almost impossible to believe that her life could have changed so drastically in such a short time. Only a couple of hours after she'd been sitting gazing at that stone family, Jessica Hart had swept her out of the Children's Aid office and taken her and her unhappiness into a world she had never dreamed would be hers. It seemed that she had been caught up in a dizzying whirl ever since.

To Min, the naked people still looked cold. She dropped a step behind the others and sent a quick wave to the baby festooned with snow.

I sat right there and hoped for a miracle, she remembered, and I got one!

As they waited to cross the street, Jess told them about being taken to this church when she was six by her adoptive parents.

"I was in the children's choir, and when I was nine, I actually sang a solo on Christmas morning. I remember shaking in my shoes," she said, laughing and leading the way up the aisle.

The church was crowded and they had to sit in the second row. A large Christmas tree stood near them and Min smiled as she caught its woodsy scent.

"Do you remember the song?" Toby whispered to Jess once they had settled themselves.

"I do, as it so happens," Jess told him quietly. "It was a verse from 'The Huron Carol.' I suppose they thought it was made to order for an Indian child, although, to my knowledge, I was never wrapped in a ragged robe of rabbit skin."

Min had no idea what she meant until they sang the hymn as part of the service. It reminded her not of Jess as a child but of herself. She stood and joined in singing the words and smiled at the verse Jess had quoted:

Within a lodge of broken bark
The tender babe was found.
A ragged robe of rabbit skin
Enwrapped his beauty 'round ...

But his parents were *with* him, Min told herself. And they had not left him there alone. And the rabbit skin might not have been ragged.

When she had been fostered by Natalie Snyder, her little girl Holly had had a rabbit-skin muff, and it had been beautifully soft and not a bit ragged. Min had stroked it and longed for one just like it, even though Holly Snyder hardly ever used it. It ended up in the dress-up box.

While the rest of the service went on, Min looked up the next hymn. It was one she had never heard before, even though Enid had dragged them all to church every week and made Min go to Sunday School too. It wasn't just a song, like "Jesus loves me," but a poem with its own music. She read over the words to the first verse while they took up the collection. Some of the words reminded her of herself out in the country in front of Mabel's house, spinning around in the drifts and toppling over and ending up making her snow angel.

Reeling, clapping, touch the air
Is that fragrant music there?
As she took in the last two lines, her eyes widened.
Lost we were a grief ago.
Now we're dancing through the snow.
It was as though the person who made up the words had looked inside her and seen her imprisoned in loneliness and then, all in a blink, breaking free to dance through a field of shining snowflakes.

While the minister led them in prayer and made an announcement about refreshments, Min concentrated on trying to memorize the rest of the words. She did not understand them all, but they still sang deep inside her, bringing with them a delight she usually only experienced when she was drawing.

That afternoon they watched an old Christmas movie about Ebenezer Scrooge. After supper they played games and then, before bed, Jess turned on the television to see if a choir would sing them one last carol.

The newscast was a terrible shock. While they had been spending a pleasant Boxing Day, a mammoth tidal wave had swept up onto the shores of Asian islands and countries, killing hundreds of people and leaving thousands lost. As they watched and listened in horror, the news grew more and more alarming and tragic. Thousands of men, women and children in Thailand, Indonesia, Sri Lanka and countless other places Min barely knew existed, seemed to have been swept away or their homes had been broken and flattened under the rushing wall of water.

As facts piled up, backed by the first television pictures, Toby's face went white as chalk. Min, staring at him, learned in a flash that having your father in danger could hurt as much or maybe even more than having none.

"If Dad's all right, why doesn't he call?" Toby kept saying

in a strangled voice.

Jess did her best to persuade him that the news might still be good, but it was impossible to believe as the numbers of dead and missing continued to rise.

Min buried her face in Cassie's soft coat and whispered love words into her ears, but even though the puppy waved her tail happily and puffed breaths into Min's downcast face, her mistress was left trapped in a deep sorrow, her heart aching for complete strangers. At first she compared the orphaned children to herself. There were dozens of foundlings. But their plight seemed so much worse. There were so many of them and no Mrs. Willis waiting to look after each one. They didn't even have enough cribs for all the babies, and many were hurt.

The three of them could not go to bed until two in the morning, when even Toby's eyes began to droop with weariness. Laura called from Saskatoon, but she had no comforting word to pass on.

Toby told them that his mother figured there was always the chance that Patrick had managed to catch an earlier flight at the last minute – even though he wasn't scheduled to fly out until tomorrow. If so, he would have already started for home when the tsunami struck.

But even Min could tell that she had been unable to keep her son from guessing that she was almost as worried as he was.

It bewildered Min. How could Laura still care so much for

someone she had chosen to leave? Puzzled, she looked to Jess for answers. Her question, unvoiced, must have been clear.

Jess said quietly, "Oh, Min, at times like this, the heart doesn't pay much attention to divorce."

Finally she sent them off to their beds, promising to call both of them the minute there was any news to be told, even if it was bad.

But there was no word that night. In the morning, while they struggled to eat their breakfast, Jess warned them that it might be a long wait. "If Patrick was safe in some airport halfway home, he would call," she said. "But, Toby, your father is both a survivor and a reporter. He won't turn tail if he can help with rescuing people. He would know that we'd guess what he might be doing. We must wait and hope – and pray."

Min wished she felt sure that praying worked. She felt uncomfortable trying it. If you weren't sure what you believed, was it still okay to pray? But she had asked for a miracle, hadn't she? She tried asking over and over, "God, bring Toby's father back and please make somebody love the babies."

Over the next few days the news grew worse and the slow, agonizing hours of waiting mounted.

Cassie, who had begun to chase after a doughnut-shaped

squeaky toy Jess had given her, put her head through the hole in the middle and began charging around the living room wearing the thing like a sausage-shaped necklace and looking utterly foolish. Everyone, Toby included, burst out laughing. Then Toby realized he was laughing and gasped. Min wanted to tell him it was okay, but Jess got there first.

"If you were lost, Toby, and Patrick was out of his mind with worry, do you think he would not let himself laugh at Cassie?" she asked gently.

Toby glared at her for a second. Then he looked thoughtful. At that very moment, Cassie pounced on his dangling shoelace and fought it to the death in a fierce battle.

Toby could not resist her.

"She's such a clown," he wheezed, tears streaming down his cheeks. He collapsed on the carpet next to her and hid his wet face in her mop of fur. Min was not sure whether he was laughing or crying but, either way, she felt certain it was good for him.

Halfway through the afternoon, Min opened her mouth to suggest they go for Emily or, at least, call to check on how she was, but closed it, leaving the words unsaid. They would not want to tie up the phone line. Finally the veterinarian called Jess to say Emily was much better and they could come and get her in the morning. They would have to give her pills several times a day and treat her gently, but he was almost sure she would pull through. Now she had gotten rid of the abscess in her right front paw, she would be better off at home.

"Oh, good!" Min said. She gave Cassie an uneasy look. "Do you think they'll help each other settle?" she asked Jess.

"What?" Jess said. Then she followed Min's glance. "They'll be fine together," she said absently, "but we can't leave the house until we get some word – "

"What if we never do?" Toby shouted at her, his voice raw. "What if Dad's lost and we never find out?"

"We'll deal with that if we have to," Jess told him, her voice kind but matter-of-fact. "But I don't think that will happen. I've known Patrick much longer than you have, longer than Laura even, and I can't picture him being defeated by a tidal wave, no matter how gigantic."

Min, watching her closely, knew she was lying. Even this Patrick person could not live through being swept out to sea or battered against floating trees or … She made herself stop. And she turned her face away in case her fears showed.

Once again, they went to bed without knowing whether Toby's father was alive or dead.

The telephone call came at four in the morning. Toby almost broke his neck tumbling down the attic stairs. He snatched the receiver from Jess's outstretched hand and croaked, "Hello."

Min had come down the hall and stood watching. It felt

as though the others were on stage and she was looking on from an orchestra seat.

"How ... ?" Toby began. "When will he call?"

So it wasn't his father. Min held her breath. Now Toby was just listening, his face shining, and, after what seemed not long enough to get all the questions answered, he said goodbye.

"He's alive," he gasped, hanging up. "Oh, Jess, he's alive. That was Mark Jennings, his boss. Dad got word through to the station. He can't come home yet. He has to stay there to cover the story for the paper and the network. He's also doing what he can to help ... . Oh, Min, he's *alive!*"

Then he began to cry, great wracking sobs that left him gulping for air, fat tears rolling down his cheeks and splashing off his chin onto the T-shirt he wore to bed.

Jess pulled him into her arms and hugged him tight.

"Oh, Toby, he's fine," she said, tears running down her face too. "And so are you. Should you call your mother?"

"Mr. Jennings said he already called her," Toby gulped. "She asked him to call me. I'll bet she was crying. She told him I would want to hear it first-hand. She was right."

Min stared at the two of them and then jerked her gaze away. She felt relieved, happy and yet wounded somehow. She did not understand the jumble of emotions that jolted around inside her skull. They were all buzzing in there like stuff in a food processor turned on high. Without saying a word, she turned and ran, silently because she was barefoot, back to her room. She did not know Toby's father. She had no part in this drama. She had no father …

Then she heard whimpering as she opened her door and saw Cassie, marooned on the bed, her very own Cassie whom she had abandoned.

She forgot all about fathers.

"Oh, Cassie," she whispered. "Oh, my Cass. Here I am. I'm sorry I left you. You're the only one who has ever been all mine."

She lay curled up in a tight ball with her cheek pressed against her puppy's soft body, feeling the tail wag furiously, feeling the small tongue lick under her chin, feeling the quick heartbeat drumming against her cheek.

I must have a father, she told her puppy. But where is he? Who is he? He must be sauntering around somewhere not knowing he has a kid – and not caring. Never ever caring.

She remembered shows she had seen on TV where parents were reunited with children they had given up for adoption.

"If I ever wanted to find mine," she whispered into the soft ear, "I would have no way to begin. I don't know one thing about him. I wasn't Shirl's. And I wasn't Bruno's kid – I know that – but I don't even know who Bruno was. I couldn't bear being related to him."

"Hey, Rap, are you okay?" Toby asked from just outside her closed door.

She did not answer. He would get the message and go if she just ignored him.

But he didn't. He opened the door and stuck his head in instead. "Jess is making hot chocolate," he said. "Come on and have some. It's a celebration."

Then, as she lifted her eyes, he caught her expression and retreated a step. "What's wrong?" he said, his voice low and anxious.

And, as suddenly as it had blazed up, the grass fire of Min's anger sputtered and died, leaving only wet ash. "It's nothing," she got out, forcing her stiff lips into the shape of something like a smile. "I'm really glad your dad's safe."

"Yeah!" Toby said. "I'll feel better when I hear his voice, though."

Min got up and followed Toby to the kitchen, carrying the puppy cradled in her arms, not speaking, not trusting her voice. As soon as they had downed their drinks, in almost total silence, Jess sent them back to bed.

"We're fetching Emily home come morning, don't forget," she called after them. "So get to sleep – or you won't wake up in time."

Yawning prodigiously, they obeyed.

11

Bringing Emily Home

THEY LISTENED TO THE NEWS on the radio while they ate their breakfast. It was hard to take in. The number of people the tsunami had killed seemed to have almost doubled overnight. Houses, whole villages, were gone. There were so many wives searching for husbands, mothers looking for children, babies who seemed to belong to nobody.

"I wish I could do something," Min said, turning down the volume for a moment.

"So do I," said Jess. "We'll go by the Red Cross office on our way to Jack's and make a donation. That'll be a start. If you've finished, dump the dishes in the dishwasher and get your coats. I've called Jack to remind him we're coming."

Min's heart leapt and then, as she looked down into Cassie's comical face, sank into her shoes. She wanted to go for Emily, but the thought of leaving Cassie behind made her feel like bursting into tears. Maybe the puppy should come too and meet Emily at the clinic. She asked Jess.

"No," Jess said firmly. "Emily is going to have a hard enough time adjusting once she gets here. Cassie will be fine with Maude Motley watching over her. You are very motherly, right, Maude?"

Maude looked down at Cassie as though she were looking at a lower life form – a slug, maybe – and sniffed. Even Min giggled.

When the car stopped in front of the clinic, Min's stomach tightened into a knot of worry. What if Emily had not made it after all and, when they went in, the doctor would be waiting to tell them gently that it was better this way?

But Dr. Miller was watching out for them. Before he went to bring Emily out, he told them all her troubles. She had rotten teeth. He thought she had colitis. She had an infected paw. And she was severely malnourished.

"How old do you think she is?" Jess asked.

"Three, maybe. It's hard to tell. This little creature has had a very rough time. She's even been pregnant, but I doubt the puppies lived. It was not so very long ago either and she was in no condition to be bred. Anyway, she's much better now, but I must warn you … she's a frightened dog. She doesn't trust people – you'll soon see. She has been half-starved and then lost the pups and then been badly hurt. I found what I think are teeth marks from a coyote or a large dog. Anyway,

140

the bad time is over. Let's start her on her new life."

He led them into the back and lifted a small, quiet dog out of the cage where Emily had lain. Min gasped. Emily had changed so much. And yet she looked so small still, and so frail.

After being with Cassie – bouncing, bright-eyed and filled with curiosity and devilment – Min was shocked to her core by Emily's stillness. She stood and stared until the veterinarian said, very gently, "She's yours, isn't she, Min? Would you like to take her in your arms?"

Min hesitated a fraction of a second. Emily looked so fragile. Then she gently lifted the small, too-quiet dog and held her close, but not in the confident way she held Cassie. She felt afraid of hurting her. But, safe in Min's arms, Emily suddenly wagged her tail hard. She did not raise her eyes to the girl's face, but gazed past Min into the distance. Only her tail signaled recognition.

"Hello, little Em," Min whispered to the top of her head. "Nobody will hurt you now."

They were soon back in the car with medication and instructions on feeding her and treating the paw, which was no longer filled with pus but was still sore. Nobody said much. Even Toby, peering at the strange dog, was quiet.

When they entered Jess's house, Cassie was just inside the door, bouncing up and down and giving little cries of relief and excitement. She seemed to have believed they would never, ever come back. She was overjoyed to see them again.

Catching sight of Emily, Maude Motley shot up the cat tree in the living room and turned her back. She stared out the window and looked as if she were waiting for them to remove this new thing and apologize. Clearly she had not recovered from the shock of Cassie's arrival and was not at all keen on another interloper being introduced.

"Do you think I should just put Emily down on the floor?" Min asked, uncertainly. Cassie's leaping around might well frighten shy Lady Emily out of her already scattered wits.

"Sit down on the rug and keep her on your lap while you let them meet. Keep your hands low so they don't come in between them and let's see what happens," Jess advised.

Min seated herself, cross-legged, and loosened her hold on Emily, who was trembling violently. She opened her mouth to say soothing words when the little dog half-fell, half-scrambled onto the floor and fled in behind Jess's big chair, where there was a dark corner. She scuttled in as if she wanted a place where she could hide away for the rest of her life. "It's all right, Emily," Min crooned, crawling after her.

Emily did not even turn her head. She stayed absolutely still. No matter what was said to her, no matter what food was offered, she did not stir. She crouched there all morning. When Cassie went after her and sniffed at her, she gave a tiny growl, but it was hard to hear.

Jess looked at Min's stricken face. "Do you remember yourself when you first went to Robin Randall's house?" she asked.

Min stared up at her, wide-eyed. She did remember. She had refused to speak. She had pushed her head in under the pillow on her bed and she had not made a sound until a long time had passed.

"What did she do?" Toby wanted to know.

"Just what Emily is doing," Jess said quietly. "I think maybe we should do our best to pretend Emily's not there, for a while, and see if Cassie can win her over. Puppies are powerful persuaders."

All three of them had trouble ignoring Emily, though. First Min would go over with a bit of cheese. Emily seemed not to know the girl was there. She clearly had never met cheese, let alone eaten it. Ten minutes later, Toby tried some ham. Emily seemed unaware of both him and his offering.

"She's not a dog at all," Toby blurted, losing patience. "I've never heard of a dog refusing meat — especially such a bag of bones."

Jess gave him a long look.

"When I brought you home from the hospital, I had to coax you to swallow an ounce of your formula. You didn't seem to understand how eating worked," she said quietly. "You had been given your bottle in the incubator by gloved hands seemingly unattached to anyone. I talked to you and I sang to you and I played tapes to you and you grew, in that box. When you finally weighed over four pounds and I was allowed to bring you home, you would have no part of being held in my arms at first. I was worried sick."

Min was fascinated by the story. She stared at the two of them, understanding better the special feeling they showed when their eyes met.

Toby dropped at Jess's feet and tipped his head back so he was looking up at his godmother. "I'll bet I was a fast learner, though," he teased. "You can cuddle with me any time."

She laughed and pushed his head away from her knee. "Not all that fast," she told him. "I aged a couple of years during those first weeks. You were worth taking time over, though. And Emily will be too. We must just make haste slowly."

"Oh, look," Min said, pointing.

Cassie had pushed in next to Emily, curled up in a ball and yawned. A moment later, she was snoring softly. And Emily's tail was waving to and fro as she bent her head to give the puppy's ear a nervous lick.

"Oh," Toby started. "They're …"

"Adorable," Min breathed.

"I had a feeling Cassie would make the first breakthrough," Jess said. "But don't imagine Emily is over all her trauma. If Cassie pushes her a bit, that's all to the good. Older dogs are almost always patient with puppies."

They all had Christmas books to read so they busied themselves, watching the dogs with sideways glances.

When Cassie awakened, she came bouncing out of Emily's dark corner, but Emily still did not follow.

Min brought a dish of Emily's food to her hiding place.

"Wait, Min," Jess said. "Maybe this is a good moment to take Emily out to the kitchen. Let's try feeding them together. You bring the food, calling Cassie, while Tobe fetches Emily. Be prepared for her to shiver and try to escape."

It was a good thing she warned him, because Emily, who had seemed so passive, started struggling so wildly when Toby picked her up that he had trouble holding on.

Cassie had no such qualms. The moment Min put her food bowl down, the puppy instantly plunged her flat, black face into it. Min put Emily's dish next to Cassie's and stood back, and Toby began to lower Emily toward the dish.

"Min, she's going to bolt," Jess said, watching. "We'll have to start by hand-feeding her."

Emily landed awkwardly and skidded on the tile floor, despite all Toby could do to calm her. She looked terrified. Min sank down next to her and held out some of the kibble, softened with warm water, on her palm. Emily took a tiny nibble and backed away.

"I think she wants to get it away from Cassie to eat it," Toby said.

Min moved closer to Emily. The dog immediately turned her back on everyone and gobbled her single grain of kibble. Min held out more. Emily backed away from the hand as though it held something dangerous, but when Min stayed absolutely still, she made a small dash, grabbed another bit and faced away from them again while she gulped it down with frantic haste.

145

"No you don't, Cassie," Toby said suddenly.

Min's head jerked around, outraged at his scolding her darling, only to see Cassie calmly helping herself to the food left in Emily's dish.

"Heavens! How will we ever get food into her if it takes all three of us, and even then Miss Cassie is too quick for us," Jess said, helpless with laughter.

Min stared up at her. What would she do if they could not work out the problem?

"Don't look so worried, Min. I don't give up on children or dogs," Jess told her. "I think we'll have to give Emily a couple of extra feedings. She needs a lot more meat on her bones. You can practically cut your hand on them."

It was a strange day. They ended up listening while Jess read aloud. While she did, they took turns sitting quietly close to Emily, reaching out slow, gentle hands to stroke her. Cassie kept romping over, coaxing her to come and play, but she settled at last, as though she were enjoying the story too.

Min loved the book. It was called *Sandry's Book*, the first of four with the overall title Circle of Magic. It started with Sandry shut up alone in the dark, with nobody knowing she was there. Min, tensing with fear for her, found herself locked up again in the darkness of the closet at Bruno's – just like in her nightmares. When help finally came to Sandry, Min felt a weight lift from her own heart.

Emily at last ate more and, when they carried her outside, she relieved herself as though she were used to using the snowy outdoors as a bathroom. Cassie raced around, plunging her small face into the cold white stuff and then shaking it off, so that her head and flying ears were constantly the center of a small cloudburst.

"She's like one of those snow globes the Dittos have," Toby laughed.

Cassie was a born clown, keeping her game going while they all laughed at her and applauded. When they were done, Cassie trotted in after Min but Emily, although she started to follow, froze at the sight of the small back step. No coaxing could make her step up and enter the house. Toby tried luring her with kibble, but she just stood, quaking, staring off into space.

"You know what," he said, "she never looks at us. She stares past us."

"I think many dogs don't like to meet a steady gaze," Jess said. "But you're right. She never looks at people. I wonder if she sees us."

"She sees Cassie," Min said.

Toby bent to lift Emily up the step. The moment he raised her paws off solid ground, she began to thrash around again, desperately fighting to get down.

"Easy does it, Em," Toby said quietly into her soft ear. Then he looked at the others.

"What is it?" Jess asked.

"I think somebody must have picked her up and then dropped her instead of putting her down carefully. She's afraid

I'm going to let her fall."

He set the little dog down gently despite her terrified struggling.

Jess shook her head. "You could be right," she said softly. "But we'll teach her to trust us in time, poor baby."

Min ran after Emily, who was heading back to her hidey-hole.

"Don't chase her, Min, or she might grow even more afraid of people," Jess warned.

Min knelt on the carpet and stretched out her hand to where she could touch the quivering dog. "It'll be all right, Emily," she crooned. But her voice broke.

"Don't worry, Min, she'll come around eventually," Jess said as she picked up her book and sat back in her chair. "Ah, sitting here reading is a perfect activity for today."

Toby shot a look at Min that she could not understand. A few minutes later, while Jess read on, a piece of paper came fluttering down next to her. *My cousin will take us there on Friday*, it read.

Min stuffed it into her pocket. What with Cassie's coming and the news from Asia, she had practically forgotten their plans to go looking for the puppy mill. Just thinking of it made her shiver. But she was glad, too, that Toby had taken over planning the adventure.

"What will we do with the dogs when we all have to go out?" she asked, interrupting the reading.

Jess looked up, surprised.

"We could shut them up in the kitchen where there's a tile floor," she said. "I have two quilted dog beds I picked up from the woman who sold me your Cassie."

"Good," Min said, her cheeks growing hot as she realized she had interrupted the reading. "Sorry I butted in."

"Lunchtime anyway," Jess said, putting *Sandry's Book* down. "Let's see if we can get a little more food into Emily at the same time."

Cassie jumped up, tail wagging enthusiastically.

Jess chuckled. "Obviously Cassie would be glad to help Emily learn the art of eating. Just lead her to the food."

Min, watching Emily backing away from her dish until Cassie had left it and then timidly approaching it, said suddenly, "I bet she's hardly spent any time with people. If she came from that puppy mill place Mabel told you about, she would have spent all her time with a bunch of dogs, but hardly any humans. And when they did come near her, maybe it would be to do something … I don't know … mean."

"I think you might be right," Jess said, watching the dogs. "They might have given her worm medicine, and she had shots, I bet."

When they were settling down again, Toby said casually, "Oh, Jess, Martha invited Min and me to go tobogganing with her and a couple of her friends on Friday. Is that okay with you? We'd be back before supper."

Jess studied him for a long moment.

"It sounds great," she said dryly, "but, as I said, I thought you despised Martha. The sudden change of heart is a bit unexpected."

"As I said, that was when I was younger," Toby shot back. "I'm mature now. Besides, she has a car."

"Just see that you both come home safe and sound, and it's fine with me," Jess said. "But be careful, Toby. You are not to take chances with my girl."

"I wouldn't," Toby said, giving her a look as angelic as his little sister Grace's.

Min bent her head down to peer at the dogs. She was also hiding another blush, this time one of pure delight. *My girl*, Jess had said.

12

Walking into Danger

NEW YEAR'S EVE FELL ON FRIDAY, but neither Min nor Toby were thinking about celebrating that evening. They stood just up the road from the end of Mabel's drive and waved as Martha and her friend Joanie pulled away.

"I'll pick you up right here at about three," she had said. "I have to get the car back to Mum by four."

"We'll be here," Toby assured her. They kept smiling and waving. They saw no need to tell her that Jess had dropped the news that Mabel was in Peterborough visiting her sister.

"Least said, soonest mended," Toby quipped, quoting a saying Jess often used.

"Let's go down the hill at least once," Min said, trying not to reveal the fact that she had never gone tobogganing in her life. Her foster families had watched sports on TV. She had seen hockey and figure skating and Olympic athletes flying high on skis. But she had never taken part in any winter sport herself. She had had plenty of snowballs thrown at her, but those did not count.

"Sure," Toby said. "Maybe we can make two or even three runs before we turn into detectives."

As they swooped down the hill, Min felt a fountain of intense joy spring up inside her. The blowing snow was needling her cheeks and she had to gasp for breath because the air was so cold. But it was far more exciting than she had imagined. Toby steered them too close to a smallish evergreen tree that seemed to arrive from nowhere, but he managed to miss it – if just barely. When they skidded to a stop, she tipped her head back and yelled, "Again!"

They swooped down four times before they could make themselves stop.

"We can go along the edge of the woods," Toby told her, picking up the toboggan's rope and beginning to trudge through the drifts.

"I think it's not too far away," Min said, catching up. "We heard barking when we were at Mabel's and she complained about them being across the creek on the other side of the valley."

The snow was so deep it slowed them down. After a few minutes, they settled for walking on the road partway. Then they were looking down into a valley where the sound of barking rang through the trees. As they stood, listening, a yelp of pain or fear reached their ears and they stared at each other, shocked, each struggling to hide the panic both felt.

"How will we get in to see?" Toby whispered as a man's angry voice shouted indistinguishable words.

"I can ask for a drink of water," Min told him. "I have that bit all planned."

"You are one cool customer, Rapunzel," he said, grinning at her. But he still looked shaken.

She was worried herself. The man had sounded in a rage at something or someone. Was he the one who had dropped Emily so that she was afraid to be picked up? She swallowed and mumbled, "Let's go."

Then the two of them came to the end of a lane, which had to be the one. Side by side for courage, they turned down the unpaved drive. Ahead of them, dogs yammered and whimpered, barked and growled. It sounded like a crowd scene in a horror movie called *The Dogs*. Min had watched *The Birds* at Natalie Snyder's with the older children who were being fostered there, and had had nightmares afterwards. She shivered, imagining in a split second what would happen if wild dogs took over the earth.

She felt her mouth go so dry that she really needed the drink of water she was about to ask for.

"What do you kids want in here? Get out! This is private property," a man's voice bellowed at them.

They could not see him at first. Then he came out from behind a trailer hitched to a large truck. He was massive, but his face was hidden behind goggles and a hood pulled low. His mouth and chin were also covered by a dense, matted beard.

"I just ... wa–wanted to ask for a drink," Min faltered.

"Eat some snow and beat it. We don't need kids nosing around here."

"Don't yell at them, Roy," a woman called from the house door. "They're just children."

"Kids can be spies," he growled. Then he reached up into the cab of the truck and pulled out a shotgun. He raised it as though he was about to aim it at them and blast their heads off. In spite of herself, Min let out a squeak of terror. The man slid the rifle into the roof rack, fastened it down and laughed. It was a cruel laugh, like Bruno's. The same laugh had sounded over and over in her worst nightmares.

"Who sent you here?" he demanded.

"Leave them be, Roy," the woman said. "They're not hurting you. I'll get you a drink, kids."

She had frowsy brown hair that hung low over her eyes and down past her shoulders. She smiled at Min and, although it was a nervous smile, Min found it reassuring. She was still wearing her housecoat! She kept shooting sideways glances at the man.

She's afraid of him, Min thought. So am I.

"They don't want a drink. They're leaving now! Beat it right now, both of you, or you'll be sorry," he snarled.

Both Min and Toby had started backing up when they first heard him speak. Min was no longer thirsty. Her knees felt as though they were made of jelly. Toby's face, usually pale, had grown as white as the snow on the hill.

He had his head lowered and his hand, gripping the toboggan rope, was shaking.

"Do you want water?" the woman called after them. But she did not say it as though she hoped they would answer yes.

"No. We're going. Come on, Tobe," Min muttered.

Then, moving as though they were one child instead of two, they turned and ran, the toboggan clattering up and down behind them.

The man gave a roar of laughter. "Look at them go!" he said. "Like scared rabbits."

Then the house door slammed and dozens of dogs, already growling, began to bark hysterically.

Out of sight of the house, Toby and Min slowed a bit to catch their breath, but speeded up again as soon as they could. In minutes they reached the road. Min bent over, trying to ease the pain in her side. She was shaking and gasping from a mixture of terror and a weakness that made her knees feel like buckling beneath her. Gummy worm knees, she thought.

"This way," Toby said, turning his back on the route leading to Mabel's house. "I think there's a little cottage up here somewhere. If nobody's there, we can at least hide. I saw it when Jess and I were out here getting pumpkins for Halloween. I think she knew whoever owns it."

Min stumbled after him without a word. She was losing hope of ever finding refuge. She kept making herself go on for what seemed miles, and then they rounded a bend and there was the cottage, set back in a clump of snowy evergreens.

"I hope somebody's home," Toby said, going to the door.

Min hoped so too. She felt frozen to the bone. Her teeth were chattering, partly from the icy wind and partly from fear that the man would come after them. He had seemed to positively enjoy frightening them, and he might want to chase after them and terrorize them some more. He had seemed even scarier because his eyes were invisible behind the dark goggles.

Toby lifted the brass knocker and hesitated. Then he banged it twice and waited, holding his breath.

"Come in. Please, come in," a woman's voice called.

Min's eyes met Toby's. Something was wrong. She felt dread tightening every muscle. Did he feel the wrongness too?

But Toby straightened his shoulders, whacked her on the back to encourage her – and himself – and turned the doorknob.

As the door swung wide, Min peered into the shadowy hall. Nobody was there.

"I'm out here," the voice called. "Thank fortune you've come, whoever you are. I think I've stranded myself and I was afraid I was stuck here for the duration."

Leaving the toboggan outside and wiping their snowy boots, Toby and Min followed the voice and were startled to discover an elderly lady in a bright scarlet jogging suit standing on her kitchen counter. Then they saw the lightweight stepladder that had fallen over on the floor, and her predicament became clear.

"Oh, my," Min said, staring up at the crinkled old face smiling down at them. Whoever she was, her eyes were as blue as Toby's. Her hair was flyaway and as white as spun sugar. And she looked tired, as though she might topple over any minute.

Toby picked up the stepladder and stood it where it could easily be reached. Then he went up a couple of steps and held out his hand to help her down. She clutched it gratefully and, holding fast first to his hand and then to his shoulder, slowly backed down to the floor.

"How long were you stuck up there?" Min asked, bringing a chair and placing it where the woman could collapse onto it.

"What a thoughtful pair you are!" the woman said, breathlessly. She sank onto the waiting chair and beamed up at Min. "I didn't know what to do. My balance isn't good any longer. I thought I had placed the stepladder on its feet, but the minute I stepped off it onto the counter, over it went."

"It could happen to anyone," Toby said.

The woman's eyes twinkled. "I doubt that," she said. "I think it was my lucky day that the two of you showed up at my door before I did something foolhardy in an effort to save myself. Now, what are your names and how can I help you? … No, take off your coats and boots first and you can make yourselves some hot cocoa. You look frozen to the bone."

Before long the three of them were sitting in her living room toasting themselves in front of a fire made with real logs. The cocoa slid down and warmed their insides and Min felt she had known Miss Hazlitt forever.

Then Toby's cell phone chirped. "Excuse me," he said, answering it.

It was Jess, of course. Min did not even have to strain to hear the angry voice. "Where in the Sam Hill are you? Martha just phoned here to say she couldn't find you and she had to give the car back to her mother. She was worried sick, especially when she discovered that nobody is even home at Mabel's place. You and Min let her think you would be at the house, apparently."

"I'm sorry, Jess." Toby started to make excuses, but Jess's voice cut into whatever he was about to say.

"I'll come for you right now if you'll give me directions."

Min heard Toby gulp. Jess was going to want to know what they were doing out here. She would never understand.

"Who is it?" Miss Hazlitt asked quietly.

"It's Jess ... Jessica Hart," Toby said.

Miss Hazlitt's smile became a wide grin. "Let me talk to her. I'll tell her where you are," she said. "Jess Hart used to be in my Sunday School class. She was the brightest one."

She took the receiver out of his hand. "Hello, Jess. It's Elizabeth Hazlitt speaking. The youngsters are at my house. I am so thankful to them. They arrived just in time to save me from a fix I had gotten myself into."

They could hear Jess's voice squawking.

Miss Hazlitt winked at them.

"You know where I live," she said into the phone. "Yes,

same place. You come for the kids when you're ready and the three of you can have tea with me. English tea. You know what that means."

The children kept listening as the women made plans. Finally Jess simmered down and agreed she would join them for "an English tea" – whatever that was. Min had never heard of such a thing.

Toby climbed up to screw in the light bulb Miss Hazlitt had been trying to replace, and came down safely. They took out her garbage. And they talked a lot – especially about Toby's father and the tsunami.

Miss Hazlitt asked Min about her family, but when Min shook her head and closed her lips tight, the old lady let the subject rest without prying or even looking surprised.

"Min is Jess's foster daughter," Toby put in, not looking at her.

Min was unsure how she felt about his volunteering this to a stranger. Yet, in the next breath, she felt relief surge up in her heart. He had not only saved her having to talk, he had said the thing that mattered.

Toby went on to tell the old lady horror stories about his twin sisters and the chaos they could create. Even Min could not help laughing out loud at their incredible exploits.

" … and then," he went on, "there was the afternoon Grace painted the bathroom wall, as far up as she could reach, in stripes of every kind of shoe polish Mum owns."

"Heavens!" Miss Hazlitt said, choking with laughter.

"Your poor mother!"

"Grace keeps telling Mum that she'll be good if they get her a dog," Toby went on.

At that Miss Hazlitt started on a new tack, one that so shocked them it stopped their conversation cold.

"I had a dear little dog myself," she said, her voice sad. "She was a tiny, cream-colored Peke stray I found outside my door one morning last month. I took her in and nursed her as well as I could. I called her Daisy."

She went on, not noticing their shocked silence as she told the story. She'd had the dog a couple of weeks before Christmas. Then, when she had it outside one day, a coyote had come racing through and snatched it up.

"There's a man who rides a big motorcycle living nearby," she went on, still not noticing their tension. "He's not a nice man, but he came roaring along just as that animal was racing away with Daisy in its jaws. He rode straight at it. I think the coyote dropped Daisy and she fled into the trees, but I couldn't find her. She left no track I could follow. She weighed next to nothing and she was such a timid little thing. I'm sure she must be dead. But it breaks my heart thinking of her. She had just begun to trust me."

Nobody said a word. Min felt she was suffocating. Should she tell?

"Where do you think she came from?" Toby asked bravely.

"I suspect she ran away from the kennel up the road. It's a puppy mill, really, but the authorities just can't seem to get it shut down. I do my best not to think about the poor animals they raise. The neighbors say they are supposed to be guard dogs, but the woman has little ones too and sells the puppies."

"We could try looking …" Toby said after a moment.

"No, no. If nobody found her, she would have frozen by this time. Let's not tell Jess. She'd be broken-hearted. Even as a little girl, she was forever rescuing lost kittens. I remember her mother shaking her head over her, saying she would end up going out and saving lost animals. Then she married Gregory and went out to help wounded people."

Like me, Min thought. She rescued me.

Her eyes met Toby's. Her own horror looked back at her, but he shook his head ever so slightly.

"You're right," he said firmly to Miss Hazlitt. "We shouldn't say a word about your losing your dog. Jess would feel awful. What did you say Daisy looked like?"

"She was a bundle of bones and her breath was terrible. I was planning to take her in to the veterinarian, but I had no way to get there. Then one day she was just gone. I only had her for about two weeks. I searched and searched, but there was no sign of her. I suppose I shouldn't have told you about it. It's too sad."

Min swallowed hard and made herself begin to talk about Christmas, the tree they had cut down at Mabel's and the books Jess had given her. Miss Hazlitt had been a school librarian, so they had plenty to discuss after that and, when Jess's van pulled up in front of the cottage, the subject of lost

Pekingese had been forgotten. Almost.

Jess greeted Miss Hazlitt warmly before she gave the kids a glare to remember. "When we get home, you will phone and apologize to Martha," she told them. "She was beside herself with worry."

Min nodded and Toby blurted out that he had been planning to do just that. Jess's face softened and it grew almost warm as Miss Hazlitt launched into the story of their finding her marooned on her counter.

After that, they all began to enjoy themselves. Hearing tales of Jess's childhood fascinated Min. She began to feel secure, no longer worried about getting into trouble. She helped get the "tea" ready. It was a large, delicious meal with lots of choices – slices of homemade bread and butter, cheese, ham, a bean salad, hard-boiled eggs that Miss Hazlitt had helped her devil, raisin buns, sardines and something strange called marmite.

But she should have realized that Dr. Jessica Hart was not one to let them off so lightly.

The minute they were in the van, her first question came at them fast and hard. "What were you two up to out here? You told me Martha was taking you tobogganing, Toby, but Martha says it was your idea, not hers, and you only asked for a ride as far as Mabel's drive."

Min sat, head down, miserable and mute. A cold fear spiraled up from an iceberg hidden deep within her. Why didn't Toby answer? It had been his idea to get Martha's help.

Toby coughed nervously. Then he cleared his throat. "I'm sorry, Jess," he mumbled at last. "Min and I –"

Then Min's courage returned and she was inspired. She burst out, "It was my idea really, not Tobe's. I had never ridden downhill on a toboggan, not once, until today. I wanted to try it and I nagged at him to arrange it. It was stupendous!"

Nobody spoke for a long minute. In that small silence, Min realized that she had blown it totally. She hated talking, let alone nagging at a boy. Jess would guess she was lying. Why hadn't she left it to Toby?

Then Jess laughed. "I love you both," she said. "And you have a right to make private plans. Tobogganing is fun. I'm glad you went for it. But I don't want you doing something dangerous behind my back and I don't appreciate being told lies. Next time, just say you can't explain. Thank fortune you had a cell phone so I could find you. I don't see why it was such a secret, and I suspect there is more to the story, but never mind. Next time, just tell where you are going and we'll forget today."

Min and Toby sighed in unison. Min bit the thumb of her mitten to keep from shrieking with relief.

"You're on," Toby said. "We're really sorry we worried you. Right, Min?"

"It led to my seeing Miss Hazlitt for the first time in years," Jess said, turning into her driveway. "She was one of my favorite people when I was a child. She helped get me out of trouble many a time. My adoptive parents were over protective and apt to pile on too many rules. I made up my mind to try not to do likewise, now that I have a child myself."

By now, Min was clutching her braid so tightly her hand ached. When she heard the last few words, she let her fingers uncurl very slightly and she began to breathe normally again.

Toby, looking back at her, saw her face go pink and her mouth widen in a slow smile. As their eyes met, he must have seen how frightened she had been before Jess's words let them off the hook. "Hey, Rap, don't sweat it," he said. "Jess's bark is not that bad, and she never bites – not hard enough to make you bleed, anyway."

"Yeah, I know," Min said. But her shaking voice betrayed her.

Jess was halfway out of the van, but she swung around and peered at Min. Then she reached her right hand back between the seats and grabbed Min's kneecap. "I think you must have forgotten my promise," she said. "I'll say it again and add a new bit: You will never leave me unless you wish to go, Min, and even if you decide you can't stand life with me another minute, I'll fight to hold onto you. You've been with me for just over a week and already I feel you've been mine always. I don't say such things lightly, either. Ask Tobe."

Before Min could take in the full sense of what she had just been told, Jess was out of the van and heading for the house.

Wordlessly, Min and Toby followed her, to be met by a leaping Cassie, a meowing Maude and no sign of Emily.

Before even undoing her coat, Min gathered her puppy up and clasped her to her chest. Cassie bounced and wiggled and licked and gave small yelps of ecstasy.

Toby laughed and bent to stroke Maude, who did her best to trip him up in her purring circles.

Jess searched for and found Emily in a dark corner of the bathroom, huddled behind the toilet. Her tail waved when Jess crouched to pet her, but she did not make a sound. And when Jess drew her out and lifted her into her arms, she did not look at any of them, but beyond them into some distant space. "Such a pretty Lady Emily," Jess crooned. "Such a beautiful Pekingese. You will feel happier soon, wait and see."

Emily ducked her head down and gave Jess's thumb one lightning lick. Then she went on pretending she did not know they had come home.

"How long will it take her to learn that we're her friends?" Toby wondered aloud.

Min said nothing, but she remembered hearing her various foster parents say, "She doesn't trust us. How long will she go on like this?"

"However long it takes, her trust will be worth winning," Jess said, looking up. And, for a split second, her smiling eyes met Min's.

"After that tea, none of us needs any supper," Jess said a few minutes later. "But I have to go to the store. And my friends Pauline and Terry have invited me in for a celebratory drink. You probably don't remember, but tomorrow is New

Year's Day."

They stared at her. She was absolutely right about their having forgotten.

"I won't stay long. Take good care of the menagerie," Jess called, pulling her gloves on.

Toby nodded and Min said, "Of course."

After she had left the house, though, a silence fell between them. Min was thinking of Miss Hazlitt and Daisy. Emily was probably Daisy. As a matter of fact, Emily was almost certainly Daisy. The veterinarian had said she had puncture wounds in her back, as though she had been bitten by another animal. That awful man in the goggles had probably saved her when he tried to run the coyote dog down. How terrifying the whole experience must have been for her!

But she's mine, Min thought. I found her.

Miss Hazlitt found her first, another inner voice answered sternly. And you have Cassie.

Stubbornly, Min shut her mind against the thought. Cassie or no Cassie, Emily needed her. Emily was hers by right.

13

Telling Toby

"WHY DO YOU CLUTCH YOUR BRAID that way?" Toby's voice demanded suddenly, breaking in on Min's troublesome thoughts.

She gripped her braid more fiercely than before. "None of your business," she flashed back, glaring at him. Why didn't he go listen to his iPod or play with his PSP?

"Cool your jets, Rapunzel," Toby said. "It was just a question, not an accusation."

Min seethed. She searched her mind for a cutting remark to hurl back at him, but her mind was like a frozen computer keyboard. It would not respond no matter how hard she hit the keys.

"You know," Toby began, lying down on the floor with his hands behind his head, "I still haven't figured out where Jess picked you up. One minute I had this godmother with no kids, and overnight she gets herself a daughter. And it seems she's known you for years. What I don't get is, where've you been hidden away all this time?"

Min did not move so much as an eyelash. It must puzzle him. In his place, she'd be driven crazy with questions. He'd been incredibly polite not to demand an explanation long ago.

But what should she say?

If he had pressed her, she would not have said anything at all. But he simply waited. His face showed he was interested, but willing to let the subject drop if that was how she wanted it.

"I never heard of you either." Min dodged answering for a few seconds longer. She had let go of her braid, but the minute she began to talk she reached for it again. Her past was not his affair, and yet she knew a lot about his past – private things about him as a baby and everything. Jess had told her right at the start. Why hadn't Jess also told Toby the story of Min's being abandoned?

Min thought she knew why.

Jess had left it up to her to tell or not to tell. The story of Toby's birth had nothing shameful or hurtful in it. But her story was different. He had been loved; she had been thrown away.

"I'm a foundling, if you must know," she said finally, in a voice just above a whisper.

Toby sat up so fast he startled her. "Like Oliver Twist?" he asked, his eyes bright with excitement.

Min had seen the movie but it took her a moment to remember. "I guess," she said. "Only he was a baby, right? And his mother took him to the poorhouse or wherever? I was about three when I was found."

Toby was leaning toward her, as though she were telling him a spellbinding tale. She had not thought of it like that but, all of a sudden, it became filled with suspense to her too – suspense and sadness and a puzzle nobody would ever be able to solve. And, just maybe, a happy ending.

"Where did she find you?" he asked in a voice close to a whisper.

"She didn't. I was left in a washroom at the CNE," she told him. "This woman – her name was Shirl – took me to the washroom and, while I was peeing, she just took off. She wasn't my mother. She told me so herself."

"When you were younger than my sisters?"

"That's right."

There was no glimmer of laughter in his face. He was clearly deeply shocked. He also looked furious, his face flushed, his blue eyes blazing.

He jumped to his feet and glared down at her. "How could she?" he yelled. "How could anybody do such an awful thing? It's evil!"

Min gazed up at him. She felt as though a tight rope had been knotted around her heart for years, without her being aware of it, and now Toby's fury had cut through its strangling cords. Nobody had ever said before that what Shirl had done to her had been wicked, but she had always known it. It was not her own fault. Jess had made that clear. But even she had never put the blame squarely on the woman who had deserted a small child, leaving her with no friend, no food, no protector, no place to turn.

Tears slid down Min's face without her even noticing them. "Yes," she said quietly. "Yes. It was a bad thing to do. I was so lonely and so frightened. And, before she took me there, she cut all my hair off as short as ... as a dog's. It was practically as short as Maude's."

He looked at the long braid that she now held in both hands, as though he were seeing it for the first time. "Why would she do that?" he whispered.

"I think ... I think maybe it was so the man we lived with wouldn't know me ... if there was a picture in the paper. He was worse than her, way worse."

"I see," he said. "I get it now."

And she thought perhaps he really did.

"They put me into foster homes," she told him, unable to stop now that she had started. She summed up the rest of her life in a hurry. "The foster parents kept giving me back. Mrs. Willis was going to find me another placement when Jess swept in and kidnapped me right out of the Children's Aid office. She said she knew all about being abandoned because it had happened to her, and then she brought me home. She's a friend of my caseworker and she knew my first foster mother too. I think she's worked for the Children's Aid before. Was she a foster parent for sick babies or something … ?"

The corners of Toby's lips quirked up. "Yeah," he said. "She took in babies they thought might die. She took me for a while." Then, "You mean, she just snatched you without any warning?" He started to laugh and dropped back into Jess's chair. "I wish I'd seen that," he said.

"I met her long ago when I was in the hospital, and I've seen her off and on, ever since. But I sure wasn't expecting her to do what she did," Min said, grinning in spite of herself. "Then, the day after she yanked me out of Mrs. Willis's office, you showed up."

"No wonder you looked at me like I was Harry Potter's Muggle cousin," Toby said. Then his face sobered. "Jess was not just abandoned," he told her, in a low voice. He was undoing his sneakers and lacing them tighter while he talked. "Her mum was a drunk and she wasn't taking proper care of Jess. So Jess's grandfather found them and said he'd take her. And her mum said, "What'll you give me for her?" And she finally handed Jess over for a case of beer. Then he took Jess home with him, but he couldn't look after her himself. And she was abused or something. I don't know the details, but she ended up being adopted."

Min stood up and ran out of the room. Toby half-rose to follow her and then sat down to wait as he heard her slam the bathroom door. Behind the door, Min was doubled up over the toilet, gagging. She thought, at first, that the wonderful English tea was going to come up, but it didn't. She was crying at the thought of a little baby girl being sold by her own mother. At least Shirl had not been related to Min herself. She had told Min so more than once.

The gagging ended at last, without the food coming back up. She spat sour phlegm into the basin and splashed cold water onto her face. When she got herself collected, she scrubbed her cheeks with a towel and took a deep, shaking breath.

Then she heard Toby coming slowly through the kitchen, clearly anxious and uncertain what to do.

"Hey, you okay in there?" he asked.

She opened the door and faced him. "Come on," she said, leading the way back to the living room. The Christmas tree would cheer them both up.

"I'm fine," she said when they were safely back there. "Let's play crokinole or watch a video maybe."

"Now you're talking," he answered. "I'll go get out the board. Jess almost always beats me. I need practice and we don't have a board at our house. Baxter asked me if I didn't think it was a bit old-fashioned. I told him it was Canadian, like Trivial Pursuit, and challenged him to a game. He laughed and turned me down. I think he was afraid I would beat him hands down."

"I'd never heard of it before I came here," Min admitted. She was lining up her men when he said in a mumbling, self-conscious voice, "You know what, you weren't a foundling. You were a lostling. Then along came Jess and found you. Your lucky day."

Min had no answer ready for this, so she simply nodded.

They played a couple of games before Jess came in. She offered to take them both on, but Min's finger was too sore to keep playing. She sat and watched and, as she did, she realized that neither of them had said a single word to Jess about a little lost dog called Daisy. Min still could not face the knowledge. Maybe Miss Hazlitt was all adjusted to doing without Daisy. She hadn't had her all that long, anyway.

She held Cassie close and knew it was not that easy to lose a beloved dog. If Cassie was stolen from her tomorrow, the loss would leave a jagged hole inside her, a hole Emily could not fill, even though Cassie had not been hers for as long as Daisy had been Miss Hazlitt's.

They would have to tell. She had known it all along. But maybe Miss Hazlitt would want them to keep Emily now that she had such a good home. Min held onto the hope with the same tenacity with which she clung to her braid.

And they needn't tell tonight.

She willed herself to switch off her uncomfortable thoughts and sleep. But she woke at midnight to hear car horns blowing and church bells in the distance. A new year had begun. She sat staring out at the snowy night and then she laughed.

Next year could never match the one just past for excitement, she thought. I resolve to …

But her eyes closed again and she made no New Year's

resolution at all.

14

A New School

"MY MOTHER'S COMING BACK TOMORROW,"
Toby grumbled on New Year's morning. "She reminded me,
on the phone, that school is about to start up again."

Min had forgotten about school. It had been almost two
weeks since she had gone to Mrs. Willis's office with Enid
Bangs. And so much had happened in the meantime. She had
a totally new life. Must she ruin it with school?

"Sybil asked me if you want to stay in the school you've
been attending," Jess said. "But I have a feeling you might like
to make a fresh start there too. Am I right?"

Min gaped at her. How had Jess guessed how miserable
she was at school? Then it dawned on her that she had never
spoken of any girls, that she had never phoned anyone or
asked to have a friend over. She supposed it hadn't been all
that hard for a smart woman to figure out.

Up until he moved, Laird had always been the one who started the name-calling, but there were others who had followed his lead.

"The Throwaway Stray," Dawn Rushton had sneered once. "Why would we want *her* on our team?"

Most of the others had ignored this. They had ignored Min too. As a rule, they had behaved as though she were invisible or as though she were in the way.

Once Mrs. Willis had asked her about friends and, when Min growled that she had none and didn't want any anyway, she had said, "Most people make friends with people who look friendly. Could you be holding them at arm's length? Have you tried smiling?"

Min had been infuriated. She remembered the week last October, when a new girl had moved into the neighborhood. Min had liked the look of her. For one thing, she had had a longish braid that began on the crown of her head and dangled down her back. Meredith, her name was. And she had come from England. But before Min had had a chance to get to know her, the others had guided her away and whispered Min's shameful history. At least, Min supposed that was what they were whispering about. Afterwards, Meredith had hung out with Beth and Asmira.

Who cares? Min said to her bruised self. She had not lost Meredith's friendship, because she had never had it. She had just hoped. Once or twice, during November, she had caught Meredith looking at her, and once she thought she had even seen her smile, but Min had closed that door out of loneliness and was not about to risk trying to open it again.

"What school would I go to?" she asked, looking into the bright flames in the gas fireplace.

"Victory is closest," Jess said calmly. "It's at the far end of the park. It's an old school. I went there myself for a couple of years when I was a child."

Min's head jerked up. But she managed to keep her voice level and a bit bored. "That sounds okay," she said.

"I have a surprise for you. I'm going to be going to school myself," Jess announced. "I had decided to take some time off, not long before I brought you home. I was toying with the idea of starting on a new career. That might have been part of what freed me to act on impulse that day in Sybil's office. I've applied to take a couple of courses to complete my certification as a family therapist. I almost finished it last year, but I still need two more courses. I'll be attending classes at the university until the end of the spring term. Then I'll be able to work during the day and be home with you during the evenings. Perfect, wouldn't you say?"

Min laughed at her. "I'll help you with your homework," she said.

"I intend to practice everything I learn on you," Jess said.

The night before school began again, Jess knocked at Min's bedroom door.

"Come in," Min called, holding onto Cassie, who was cavorting around on the bed and in danger of tumbling over the edge.

"How would you like a new name to use at your new school?" Jess asked, smiling. "On several of your school reports, teachers call you Minerva or Minna. I know you hate Minerva, and Minna doesn't sound like you either. Look here for a moment."

Min stared at her, bewildered but curious. Jess held out several books.

"These belonged to my mother," she said. "My adopted mother, that is. They were written by an American writer called Jessamyn West. One of them I think you'd enjoy now. It's about a teenage girl called Cress Delahanty. It'll sound old-fashioned to you, maybe, but I liked it enough to read it several times. But it's her name I want you to think about."

"Cress?" Min echoed, mystified.

"No, Jessamyn. When I was young, I wished I had been named Jessamyn instead of Jessica," Jess said. "I liked the sound of it. Then the other day it came to me that it's a combination of our two names, Jess and Min – Jessamyn. If you claimed that your given name was Jessamyn instead of Minerva, you could still be Min and nobody would call you those names that rile you so. If anyone did, you could just set them straight: 'I'm not Minerva; I'm Jessamyn.'"

"Jessamyn," Min repeated, trying to take in what on earth Jess was suggesting. "Jessamyn."

178

A new name. A name to use at school. Min sighed. Never again to be called Minerva. Or Minnie!

It was such an unexpected idea that it took time to get her brain to absorb it. Jess did not keep talking. She simply waited for Min to consider the idea, to sound it out and decide for herself.

"Jessamyn," Min whispered at last, her eyes lifting and beginning to sparkle.

"I'm sorry I didn't come up with it sooner," Jess said. "But I happened to see the books just before supper, and the notion came."

"I like it," Min said. "Would it be all right if I tried it? It isn't against the law or something?"

Jess laughed aloud. "No law I know of," she said. "And if you decide you want to keep the name for life, once you've given it a fair trial, we could actually make it legal."

After she went out, Min murmured her new name over and over into Cassie's soft ear. She loved its sound and, even more, she loved the way it linked her with Jess.

The following morning, the two of them got ready to walk to Min's new school. Jess had Min's records with her – report cards and test results and all. She had shown them to Min at breakfast.

Instinctively, Min had averted her eyes from the teachers' comments. "How … ?" she started to ask.

"Sybil had copies. They were in your file. I got her to hand them over when I went to see her last week."

Then Min made up her mind to face what had been said about her. Jess had told her once that she had guts. Well, she'd prove her right. She swallowed and scanned the remarks. Almost every one made her wince.

Minerva lacks self-esteem and refuses to participate in class.

Minerva needs to learn how to work with others.

Minna has poor communication skills and is insolent at times; make an effort, Minerva.

Min is a stubborn child not interested in learning. Her tragic past is no excuse for her insolence. Mend your manners, Min.

Min seems withdrawn and I believe therapy is indicated.

Although her test scores show Minna to be intelligent, her behavior reveals scant evidence of this. Perhaps she should be retested.

Minna, you must try harder or you will end up dropping out before you finish high school. Think this over. Join in more and leave that sullen look at home.

Min seems to find school irrelevant.

That last was the Gym teacher. If she had not insisted on calling her Minna, no matter how often Min corrected her, Min would not have given her the look that they all called "insolent" and "sulky."

There were lots of *U*s for Unsatisfactory.

But there was her Art mark. A-plus. Nobody seemed to see it except Jess, who now pointed her finger at it.

"I'd like to see some more of your art," she said. "In case you're wondering where my Christmas tree picture is, it's at Wyndham Arts getting framed. Don't worry unduly about this stuff. They don't know the Min I know – and I think things will improve fast."

Framed! Min had fixed her eyes on the toes of her shoes and tried not to blush with pleasure.

The two of them entered the front office side by side.

"This is my foster daughter, Jessamyn Randall," Jess told the principal, Mrs. Wellington. She said it so smoothly Min almost missed it. "She likes to be called Min for short."

"Jessamyn?" Mrs. Wellington said. "I haven't come across that name before. It's attractive."

"Isn't it," Jess replied without a blink. "It matches the girl who bears it."

The principal studied Min. "I see that it does," she said quietly.

To her surprise, Min warmed to Mrs. Wellington right away.

Jess rose then. She squeezed Min's shoulder.

"I'll leave her in your capable hands. See you later, Min."

When she was gone, the principal looked around for someone to take Min to her new homeroom: Ms. Spinelli, Grade Six.

"It's a split Five/Six," Mrs. Wellington said. "Oh, there's

Penelope! Penny, would you please take Min with you and show her where Ms. Spinelli's room is. You'll be in the same class."

"Sure," the girl said.

They walked down the hall together. When they reached the foot of the stairs leading up to the second floor where the classroom waited for them, they stopped and studied each other.

Penelope was brown-skinned and small. Her black hair was long and curled up at the ends. Her dark eyes were friendly. Her flashing smile looked as though she meant it. "Did she say your name was Minerva?"

"No," Min said, fighting to keep her new smile in place. "She said Min. It's short for Jessamyn." She waited for a reaction.

"Nice," Penny said. "I'll call you Min unless you make the mistake of calling me Penn-elope."

Min relaxed. She laughed. "I won't," she said and they began to climb the stairs.

Ms. Spinelli was surprised to learn she had another girl in her class, but she was pleasant about it. "Do you go by Jessamyn or just Jess?" she asked.

Min almost changed herself into Jessamyn then and there, but she realized in time that she might not remember. So much else was new that day. "I'm Min," she said simply.

"Very good, Min," the teacher said. "There's an empty desk in the second row. Try it out for size this morning. We can make a final decision later. Penny's desk is right across the aisle."

Min turned to see how Penny felt about this and found that her smile had widened into a happy grin.

"Follow me, kid," she said and led the way.

Ms. Spinelli went back to writing something on the chalkboard.

"Where were you before Christmas?" Penny asked.

"Paisley School. But I'm living on Glasgow Street now."

"Do you have brothers and sisters?"

"No," Min said, looking down at the ballpoint she was getting out of her pencil case. "But I have a nine-week-old Pekingese puppy named Cassie."

"Wow!" Penny said, looking impressed. "I have two big brothers and three little sisters. My mother says we can have pets when we can look after them. We did have a hedgehog, but he escaped and got lost in the basement. When my little sister found him, Mum made us give him to our cousins. They're more organized."

"Was he nice?" Min wanted to know. She'd never known anyone with a pet hedgehog.

"My sisters thought so, but I wasn't all that keen, to be honest. He had really sharp quills and he hissed. I was scared of him – although I never admitted it."

Min laughed out loud and Penny chuckled.

Then Mrs. Wellington's voice boomed, "Good morning, students," over the loudspeaker and they all stood up for the national anthem.

While they sang, Min glanced back at the class. Some of

them were staring back. Then she saw, through the open door, a boy running past. Laird Bentham!

Min stiffened. What was *he* doing here? She knew his family had moved, but surely he couldn't be going to Victory now. Min had thought it was her lucky day when he'd left Paisley School.

"What's the matter?" Penny whispered.

Min hesitated. Then she asked, "Does that Laird Bentham go to this school?"

"Yeah, worse luck," Penny answered, rolling her eyes. "He started coming here in November. He's in the other Grade Six and he's bad news."

"Tell me about it," Min muttered, opening her binder.

"Min, please come up and get a math book and a copy of the novel we are studying. Penny, I believe you have work to do … "

"Yes, ma'am," Penny said, ducking her head down over her book and snatching up a pencil.

Once everyone had settled and Ms. Spinelli had introduced Min, she said quietly, "I am sure you have all been deeply shocked about the devastation caused by the tsunami. I thought perhaps, if we all put our minds to work on it, we could come up with some way our class could raise some money to send to help the people. We should consider carefully. We would want to do our best. Everyone think hard and we'll brainstorm about it tomorrow morning. We'll begin by collecting everyone's ideas, so be sure to come prepared."

Min was glad the teacher was thinking of the people who

were suffering, but she was uneasy at the thought of doing something to make money. She could not come up with anything she was good at. She liked drawing and had always gotten her best marks in Art, but that was not something to sell.

Then Penny's whisper reached her. "If we put on a concert, you and I might sing a duet or something."

Min stared at her new friend in horror. Sing! In front of a lot of people! She had never dreamed of doing such a thing and she was sure she would make a total mess of it if she agreed to try. Yet maybe a duet would not be so bad as having to sing alone. In Min's opinion, her singing a solo would be a catastrophe. I'd die first, she told herself.

When it was time for morning break, she found herself walking out with Penny and a stringbean of a girl named Jennifer.

"Jen, come over here," Penny said.

Going along, Min felt slightly sick. What was Penny going to say?

"Min hates Laird too," Penny muttered, tugging Min into an out-of-the-way corner. "Tell us why, Min. And we can tell you what *we* think of the toad."

Min had a hard time starting. She did not want to begin new friendships by confiding the things Laird had yelled at her. She wanted to leave those nicknames behind. But, bit by bit, she got out enough of the truth for them to pick it up and start telling her what they thought. Nobody liked him.

"He calls me Gingersnap," Penny said, her eyes flashing. "And Chocolate Chip. But he whispers and he never gets caught. I've tried telling Mrs. Wellington, but she just sighs and asks if I don't think I could handle it myself. As it is, he's sent to the office almost every day by somebody."

"He's a worm," Jennifer declared. "Like a giant slug – or do I mean a giant sloth? Whatever."

Min almost laughed out loud. "Giant sloths are extinct," she said. "At least, I think they are."

Jennifer snickered. "Okay, he's not extinct, but he is a stinker. And if he doesn't watch it, one of these days he'll be on the endangered species list and nobody but his mother will lift a finger to rescue him."

"He pushed Alessia's little brother face down into a snowbank the week before the holidays," Penny put in. "The kid isn't even in kindergarten yet and now he's afraid to go outside by himself. I told my cousin and he promised to tell me a way to teach Laird a lesson. He's away, but the moment he comes back, I'll remind him."

Min hoped it would happen. But she still managed to stop short of telling them Laird's nicknames for her. She hated them and they weren't true.

"Where do you guys live?" she asked instead, amazed at how easily she was talking to kids her own age, nice kids. She had hardly ever exchanged friendly words with one other girl, let alone two. Had being Jess's foster daughter changed her somehow, made her braver? How? She saved the question to think about in bed.

Both girls lived not far from Jess's house. Jennifer, her brother Pete and their parents lived in a ground-floor apartment in an old house on Exhibition Street. Penny and her family had a whole house to themselves. It was three stories tall and yet, according to Penny, it was barely big enough.

"My sisters, my brothers and my parents have to fit into it and my auntie and her teenage daughter Cora are staying with us too, until she gets a job with enough pay to take care of renting their own place."

Jennifer hooted at Min's stunned look. "It's loads of fun over there," she said. "Her little sisters are like stair steps – three, four and five years old – and into everything. They're wild."

"They sound great," Min said, thinking of the Dittos.

"You wouldn't say so if they were your sisters," Penny said, with a sigh that fooled neither of the other girls.

"I think I saw you outside Dr. Hart's last week," Jennifer said. "You were with that boy who goes to Willow Road. Tony? Something like that. He's sure good-looking."

Min swallowed an attack of giggles. She didn't meet the other girl's eyes. Jennifer had to mean Toby. She supposed he was good-looking, although by now she knew him too well to see him the way Jennifer obviously did. Wait until she got old Tobe alone.

"His name is Toby. He's Dr. Hart's godson," she told them.

"Do you live with them?" Penny asked.

"She's adopted me," Min said boldly, shocked at how easily the lie slipped out of her mouth. Well, Jess had spoken of her as her daughter more than once. It was her fault Min was coming to believe her.

"Hey, that must be neat," Penny said. "She's a real live heroine, my mother says."

The bell rang, to Min's relief, and she rushed to line up. She felt like a balloon filled with helium, floating up into the sky. Maybe, just maybe, she was actually going to have friends. But how could she invite them over to Jess's when one of them might let slip that she had said she was adopted? If it should happen, what would Jess say?

If Mrs. Willis found out about Min's lie, she would have set the girls straight right away. But Jess was different. She had snatched Min out of the CAS office on a whim. She had said so herself, hadn't she? Or had the word *whim* come from Mrs. Willis? Anyway, Jess was a person full of surprises. You could never be certain what she would do or not do.

Seeing the complications ahead, Min longed to take the words back, but could not risk losing Penny's friendship.

When they began the brainstorming the next morning, Min found herself speaking up in a very small voice.

"Can you speak a little louder, Min, so we can all hear?" the teacher said quietly.

"I just thought we might … I guess it's dumb maybe … make it a concert of songs for the children … like lullabies or even funny ones. I don't know," she finished, flushing and wishing she had kept her mouth shut.

"We could do 'Skinnamarink' and 'Baby Beluga,'" a girl named Sally Anne said.

"My mother sings us a Punjabi lullaby," another girl murmured. "She could teach me. I think it's a great idea."

"My mum used to sing 'Sleep, my child, and peace attend thee,'" another girl offered. "It's really nice."

"Min and I are singing 'Where Is Love?' as a duet," Penny said, as though Min had promised. "My mother will coach us and play for us on the night."

"Great!" their teacher exclaimed.

"I could play 'Brahms' Lullaby' on my saxophone," Tyler said.

It was settled. Everyone thought the idea was great. Ms. Spinelli asked if someone would offer to make a poster and Min said maybe she could. Jennifer said she would too.

"I'll talk to Mrs. Wellington about a good date," the teacher said.

"I know one!" Josie offered, bouncing with excitement. "It's a while away, but it would be so perfect. Valentine's Day – A Valentine for Lost Babies."

"Start practicing," Ms. Spinelli said, smiling at them. "I think it will be splendid."

The next few days passed without the word *adoption* being mentioned, and Min calmed down. As time passed, the subject would be less and less likely to come up, and the girls might even forget what she had said.

Then Penny produced the words to "Where Is Love" from the musical *Oliver!*

"It's perfect," she said. "You can just imagine all those orphans singing it, looking all sad and wistful."

Min scowled. At last, however, she nodded in spite of herself – Penny was right; it was a great orphan song. After all, as Toby had pointed out, Oliver Twist was a foundling – just like Min.

Toby's family had come home when school began again. His father was still doing relief work and writing reports in Indonesia. Min was amazed to find that she missed Toby's living with them. The pets helped fill in the empty space though. Emily remained hidden in her dark corner most of the time, but finally began venturing out to sit in front of the floor-length mirror in the hall, gazing at her own reflection for long periods. Maude Motley watched her with curiosity and Cassie kept nosing her with what looked like anxiety. At night, Emily slept in a small, round, fleece-lined dog bed in a corner of Jess's bedroom. But she still spent most of the day hiding behind Jess's chair or staring into the mirror.

"What do you think she's seeing?" Min whispered to Jess, as they watched the mesmerized dog.

"I think perhaps she's used to seeing other dogs, but not people," Jess said slowly. "So the dog in the mirror, although it doesn't smell right, still looks like those she has known, the ones who ate first from the dog dish. I'm considering going out there and seeing what dogs they try to sell me."

"No, don't!" Min yelped, her face going stiff with fright. "That man has a gun —" She broke off abruptly and tried to ignore the way Jess was staring at her.

"How would you know that, Min?" Jess asked softly, her eyes fixed on Min's averted face.

"Mabel … " Min started and then stopped.

If only Toby were there with her, she thought, gulping. If only Jess did not seem to be looking right into the secret center of her being. If only Jess had not ordered them to keep away from that kennel!

"Mabel must have said …" she began again in a voice that did not fool Jess for a moment.

Then, like an answer to a prayer, Toby came bounding into the house. "Hey, you guys, what's up?" he demanded.

But Jess was not sidetracked by him. "Sit down, both of you," she said. "I want some answers, truthful ones."

It all came out then – their plotting, their fright, their meeting with Miss Hazlitt. Neither of them told about Miss Hazlitt's lost dog, but they told everything else.

Jess glared at them first and then shook her head. "People are always telling me I'm too trusting," she said softly. "I guess maybe they're right."

"Yeah. But listen, Jess," Toby said. "My dad's supposed to phone here in the next little while. It's easier to talk without the twins around. Can we discuss the dog place later?"

Silence lay over the room like a thundercloud. Min struggled to keep back tears. She had known, from the start, that Jess would find out someday that she was not the nice girl she believed her to be.

Then the phone rang and Toby and his father talked. Somehow, listening to the call, Min felt better. After he hung up, they filled in most of the gaps.

"Great," Jess said finally. She glanced at Min. "Don't look so nervous, Min. I actually do understand how it happened. But I'll take a police presence with me when I pay them a visit. Now, are you having supper with us, Toby?"

"Did you say you're having spaghetti?" Toby asked, licking his lips.

"I don't remember saying any such thing, but I suppose it may have slipped my mind," Jess said, and headed for the kitchen while they laughed.

Two days later, Penny invited Min to come home with her for supper. "My mother will play while we practice our song," she said.

Min did her best to act cool, as though she were forever being invited out, even though it was the very first time. They had just finished their ice cream when Penny's mother turned to look at Min and said, "I remember when you were found. What a sad story! Colleen Bentham reminded me. Did they ever discover who had left you there?"

Penny stared from her mother's expectant face to Min's frozen one. "What are you talking about, Mum? Mrs. Bentham is that awful Laird's mother. You just shouldn't listen to anything she says."

"Oh, Penny, you are too quick to judge – although I admit I am not drawn to the woman. When she reminded me about you, Min, she did say some unkind things. I set her straight, I can tell you. Penny, you are too young to remember. A little girl was abandoned in a public washroom at the Ex, years back. Nobody knew who she was and nobody came to claim her. Wasn't that how it was, Minerva?"

"My name is Jessamyn Randall," Min said at last, getting her voice to squeeze out past the hard knot in her throat. "I go by Min. But the rest is true – they never did find out who I was."

Penny gave a bounce on the couch. Her eyes were gleaming. "Min, you could be *anybody*," she cried. "A princess, a gypsy, anybody."

Min was grateful, but she knew, in her bones, that she was neither a gypsy nor a princess. Shirl and Bruno would never have been handed a princess and she was sure gypsies had black curly hair and big dark eyes. She had never met one, but that was how the ones in books looked. Her hair was a deep brown and she had dark brown eyes.

Penny stared at her, clearly dying to know more.

Thinking of her past did not hurt nearly as much as it had before Jess had swept her out of the Children's Aid office and told the veterinarian, "This is my foster daughter." All the same, it wasn't just a story in some book. She was real and she was not a gypsy or a princess either.

She was just Min.

"No, they never did find out. But I don't like to think about it," Min said, not looking straight at Penny or her mother. "Penny is right about Laird, though. He's meaner than … than a black widow spider. Now I'd better go."

"Wait until we practice our duet," Penny said. "I already set the music on the piano, all ready."

Min, half rising, sank down again.

"Mum promised to play for us, didn't you, Mum?" Penny demanded.

Min thought she might throw up, but Penny's mother rose and went right to the piano in the corner of the family room. Without stopping to talk it over, she began playing "Where Is Love?"

Penny was a strong singer, which was a relief. Min trailed along half a beat behind.

Penny's mother said Min would grow more confident. "You have a nice voice," she said. "It will just take practice on your part to bring it out."

"I guess," Min said doubtfully.

Penny laughed. "I'll walk you home," she said, pulling her coat down from its peg.

"I'm sorry my mother listened to that old bat," she said as they walked. "My dad says she keeps her foot permanently in her mouth, and sometimes I think he's right. But she never means any harm."

"Forget it," Min mumbled. "It doesn't matter. I like your mum."

She did, too. Penny's mother had spoken when she shouldn't, but Min knew the difference between honesty and cruelty. As the two girls strolled along through the snowy afternoon, dimming into dusk, they did not speak again for a couple of blocks. Then Min looked across the lawn and saw Grace and Margaret in front of Jess's house. They were leaping and whirling, kicking up a cloudburst of snow.

"Look," she said softly. "They're Toby's little sisters. They are wicked – well, at least Grace is – but very cute. They're dancing through the snow."

The twins spotted them but did not come running. Instead, they let themselves fall flat on their backs and waved their arms up and down and made their legs move like scissors opening and shutting, creating snow angels.

"Are we too old, Penelope?" Min asked in a low voice.

"No way!" Penny shouted.

And the two girls ran across the white expanse to add two

more snow angels to the much smaller pair the Dittos had made.

Cassie, gazing at them from the window, almost turned herself inside out with excitement as she watched their bewildering acrobatics.

"Don't worry, Cassie," Min called to her. "We're coming in."

That night the bad dream snatched her again and trapped her in its terror. She was using every ounce of strength she possessed to escape, but no matter how hard she tried to move even her little finger, she was paralyzed. And Bruno was coming.

"Litter-Bin Min," he jeered in Laird Bentham's voice. "Throwaway Girl. Minnie Mess."

Then Cassie, frightened by Min's moaning, began to bark, calling to Jess to come. Min awoke in her foster mother's arms, held close, and heard Jess's voice crooning, "It's all right, darling. Nobody can get you away from me. You are perfectly safe. It's all right."

Min gave way to slow tears which grew into a storm of weeping. Bit by bit, she sobbed out the story of the dream and Bruno and Shirl and the darkness in the locked closet.

Then Jess, stroking Min's hair, told of her own bad dreams. "I was afraid of my uncle," she said. "He was like this Bruno, I think. My grandfather left me with him and my Aunt Rose because he felt he was too old to care for a little girl. But when I grew older, my uncle used to hurt me. When I finally told my grandfather and got him to believe me, he arranged for me to be taken away by the Children's Aid, and after my mother died, Grandpa gave his permission and I was adopted. I was seven and I was safe with my adoptive parents. But my uncle came after me in dreams for months. Years even. I have at last managed to banish him from my sleep. You will find the nightmares growing fewer in time."

"They have already." Min hiccupped. She went on listening, trusting Jess to tell her the truth. Snuggling into her warm arms, she felt peace wrap around her like sunlight after weeks of storm.

The next afternoon, while Min was in school, Jess took Dr. Miller and a policeman and one of the staff from the Humane Society and went to the kennel where they believed Emily had spent her first couple of years. On her way home, she picked up Toby and brought him back with her so she could tell them both about it.

Min listened in horror.

"Roy was there, gun and all," Jess said, her voice and her face grim. "When he saw who was getting out of the cruiser, he actually raised his shotgun, but his sister grabbed it away from him before anyone was hurt. All the same, he's safely behind bars for a bit."

"Oh, Jess," Min breathed, pale with fright.

"They made me stay in the car while they arrested him. They radioed for help and another cop took him away. His poor sister and her friend, who helps out, are deeply grateful. They have agreed to clean up their act, but they have to face charges too. The small dogs especially were in a deplorable state. A couple were too far gone to be saved. I really think his sister will be kinder to them, now that she'll be able to stop being afraid all the time. The police will probably try to get a restraining order so he can't go badger her, and the Humane Society will collect the large dogs he was training to attack. It was lucky for the dogs that he threatened a policeman with his shotgun. It made the whole thing a more serious matter." Jess shuddered as she spoke the last words.

"Ha!" Toby exclaimed. "Let's hope they really go through with it. He deserves whatever he gets."

"Tobe, we don't know for certain that Emily came from that place," Jess began.

Toby looked at Min and waited. She knew he thought she should tell. She said nothing. Her heart felt like a lead weight. So what if Miss Hazlitt had found a dog like Emily? Emily would have died in that shed if she, Min, had not fetched help.

"Min, we have to tell," Toby said.

"Tell what?" Jess snapped, her head jerking up.

"I don't … I don't think it's the same dog," Min started. She went on haltingly to tell the story of Miss Hazlitt and Daisy. She did not raise her eyes from the floor as she got the words out. She could not bear to see the look on Jess's face. This time Jess would be disgusted with her, furious even.

Jess looked from one to the other. Toby was avoiding looking at Min, and Min still did not raise her eyes from the carpet. Her face burned and her lips trembled.

"I don't blame you, Min," Jess said at last. "But we must at least take Emily over there and see what Miss Hazlitt has to say. She may tell us her Daisy was totally different, you know."

"What if … what if it is the same dog?" Min got out.

"You know the answer, Jessamyn. We'd have to give her back. Yet I believe we should wait a bit and give Emily a chance to grow stronger. I was right about there being other dogs at the puppy mill who looked just like her. There were five of them. I imagine she was trying to decide if the dog in the mirror was one of her siblings."

"Poor Em," Min murmured, tears stinging her eyes.

"Well, Min, Emily still has to be seen by Jack a few more times, and his place would be extremely difficult for Miss Hazlitt to get to. Oh, I'm probably just as guilty as you about wanting to put off the evil day, but Miss Hazlitt lives a long way from his clinic and I doubt she drives much these days."

Min dropped to the floor next to Emily, who was curled up against the side of Jess's chair. Emily backed up but she did not flee. She looked sideways at Min, trembled and wagged her plumy tail a couple of times.

"Poor, sweet baby," Min murmured, extending her open hand, palm down. "Don't be scared. You're safe now." Then to

Jess, "Do you think we should start calling her Daisy?"

"Let's call her a mixture of both," Toby suggested. "Daisy Em and Emily Daze. She'll catch on."

"No," Jess said firmly. "She's confused enough already. I doubt she knows she has a name."

Even though Min had to live with knowing Emily was not really hers, things should have been fine after that. She had Penny and Toby and even Jennifer for friends.

She had Cassie, who was all hers, and Maude, who purred like a food processor whenever Min came in. She had Jess and she had her own room. She had new clothes and books. She liked Ms. Spinelli.

But somehow there was still a piece missing.

"Don't be dumb," she snapped at herself, using a voice as tart as Jess's. "Concentrate on all the good stuff and forget everything else. Work on getting ready for the concert."

If she kept reminding herself how lucky she was, she would soon come to believe it and be rid of this last emptiness that kept haunting her. She remembered, all at once, wondering whether Grace and Margaret knew how lucky they were. She had decided they never thought about such things. They took their good fortune for granted.

She would never be able to do that. And being lucky didn't mean being always happy and contented. Being lucky just meant you were rich in things.

Once again, she thought of the Asian foundling babies she had seen on television. The concert would help, but only a little.

That evening, she began to make a sketch of an idea for the poster. She drew a sleeping baby in a woven basket floating on ocean waves. They weren't tidal waves and the baby was sleeping peacefully, but danger surrounded her. Then she penciled in lightly, *Rock-a-Bye, Baby – A Concert to Raise Money for Children Orphaned by the Tsunami.* Her lettering was crooked but it could be fixed if Ms. Spinelli and the class liked the idea. She had always thought the baby "in the treetop" was, like the baby in the statue downtown, in peril. And for the babies in Indonesia and Sri Lanka, the wind had blown until the bough broke. She stared at her picture and then quickly rolled up the sheet of paper to take to school.

"Min, that will be perfect," Ms. Spinelli said the next morning, staring at the small child fast asleep in his basket.

"I'm good at lettering," Jennifer said. "I can help, if you like."

"Great," Min answered instantly. "I can do it, but I hate the fuss."

So it was settled. And soon copies of Min's poster were to be seen all over the school and even in Trinkets and Treasures and The Bookshelf and other stores downtown.

15

Life Story

A WEEK LATER, Ms. Spinelli had to have surgery. A handsome man arrived to be their substitute teacher for two weeks.

When Ms. Spinelli told them she was leaving, she promised to be back in lots of time for the concert. "Keep practicing," she said.

"We will. Don't worry," they chorused.

All the girls but Min thought the substitute teacher was cool. He had grey eyes with long lashes, a brilliant smile and curly brown hair. He was tall, too, and his voice was very deep. "It sounds sexy," Ashley giggled.

"He's a walking dream," Jennifer said.

"Awesome!" HueLin declared at break.

"Excellent," Frannie put in. "And splendid."

But Min did not trust him. She did not know why.

Whenever he looked her way, she felt a cold shiver run through her body and she wanted to run right out the door. He was a good teacher. He didn't try to be everybody's best buddy and he didn't make fun of anybody. He could explain things clearly. Still, Min wanted Ms. Spinelli back.

Then Mr. Harmon announced their Creative Writing project – writing their autobiographies.

"You can begin with your family background," he said enthusiastically. "That's what biographers do. But what you will be doing is your own story, a memoir. You have been alive for about eleven years. Each of those years was over three hundred and sixty days long. So I don't want to hear that you have not lived long enough. You've put in thousands of days. You will find you have rich material to draw from."

He went on to show them autobiographies of famous writers, and diaries, and even collections of letters. He read bits aloud.

Min knew she would have enjoyed listening if it did not mean she would have to write about herself. How could she bear to do it? Even if he kept what she wrote confidential, as he was now promising to do, he would still read it. It was none of his business.

She hated him.

"Interview your parents and grandparents for family stories you might want to include," he was saying.

Min almost snorted.

"But my grandparents live in Calgary," Harrison said.

Mr. Harmon laughed. "You can phone, if your parents say it's okay, or send an email or a fax. Ask for pictures and stories. They'll probably be pleased to write a real letter the way people used to do in the days before computers were invented," he said. "Some old people love to put stories on tape. Try that."

He handed out pages that had "helpful headings." Min glanced over them. *Where Your Family Came From* was at the top. *What Your Grandparents Did for a Living. Have You Moved?*

Min got that far and crumpled the page into a tight ball. Then she jammed it into her pocket.

"I don't think anyone in this class is from a First Nations family," the man went on. All the time he talked, he kept smiling around at them as though he knew they were excited about this. "If you are, your family didn't come from Europe or Asia, of course. But just put in everything you know. It'll make a rich tapestry."

Min wondered what he would say if she wrote, *I know nothing*, and handed it in. He would ask her about it in front of the whole class. Or should she say, *I came from a washroom at the Canadian National Exhibition?*

Celia waved her hand in the air.

"What if you're adopted?" she asked.

Min waited, looking at the man from under her brows.

"Are you adopted, Celia?" he wanted to know.

"No," Celia said, giggling. "I just wondered …"

"If anyone is adopted, come and talk to me about it," the teacher said pleasantly. "I don't see that it would be a problem. An adopted family is still a family with stories to tell. But we can discuss it if you have difficulty."

Min saw Penny looking at her. Was that pity in her eyes?

Then the fire alarm rang.

"Oh, I forgot! It's just a practice drill," Mr. Harmon told them. "Line up quickly."

By the time they were back in their seats, the Art teacher had arrived and there never was enough time for the class to do more than think about their life stories. Not a single sentence got written that day.

When they were dismissed, Min did not wait for Penny, but ran ahead into the park and hid herself in a clump of trees where she could wait unseen. She knew Penny and Jennifer must be wondering how she was going to write her life story, but she did not want to talk about it.

"Min!" Penny called.

Min did not move a muscle.

"She must have gone on home," she heard Jennifer say.

And, peering out from between the tree trunks, Min saw them take off without her. *Good*, she thought.

Yet she knew, however she ducked and dodged, she would finally have to hand something in. She was determined not to go up after class and talk to him about her situation. Why should she? Her early life with Bruno and the women who came and went was too painful to tell about. So were most of the years in foster care. She couldn't just tell about the happy months with the Randalls. He would demand more.

Suddenly she knew why she mistrusted the teacher. It was his eyes. Bruno, the one who had locked her in the closet and sometimes even hit her, had eyes that same grey. And he had smiled too. Smiled and smiled and then knocked her or even Shirl sometimes across the room. Mr. Harmon would not slap her. If he did, he'd be fired. But she still did not trust him, not one bit.

That night she was certain she would have the dream, but she did not. She lay awake instead, tossing and turning. And finally she realized she was still filled with rage. How dared God and everybody she had ever known treat her as though she was what Laird Bentham had called her. Litter-Bin Min.

She ground her teeth and pounded the head of the bed until Cassie ran away from her and slid headfirst over the end of the mattress onto the carpet. She let out an astonished whimper.

Min started to leap to her rescue and then didn't. "You gotta learn," she told her precious puppy. "Life is rough."

Jess knocked lightly then and, without waiting, came in to see what was the matter. As she asked, she scooped Cassie up and put her back close to Min.

But Min only punched the pillow hard, turning her back, and said, "No! Everything is fine, just fine."

Jess left the room without quizzing her further. Min gathered Cassie into her arms but still lay dry-eyed and stiff with a fury she only dimly understood.

"They all piss me off," she told the squirming puppy. "None of them really knows. Whatever Jess says, nobody understands."

In the morning, Min said her throat was sore and her nose was stuffy and she felt too sick to go to school.

"Let me take your temperature," Jess said.

"No. I'm sick and I'm not going to school whatever you say!" Min yelled. She spun around, ran back into her room, slammed the door and dove back under her quilt.

Jess followed her, sat on the edge of the bed and watched the back of Min's head for what seemed like years. Then she said, very quietly, "Well, we all need time off every so often. Let me know if you want to talk about it. Or when you feel well enough to go back."

"My throat really is sore," Min called after her, doing her best to sound croaky.

"See you at lunchtime," Jess answered calmly and left the house.

Penny phoned when she got home. Min called out that she was too sick to talk. Jess came in with juice and cheese and crackers for her. Min ignored them until Jess left and then gobbled down every crumb. She stayed home for the rest of the week. Jess did not say much, although she finally insisted on taking Min's temperature.

"It's a miracle," she exclaimed, shaking the thermometer dramatically. "Your raging fever has gone. You're cured."

Her laughing eyes met Min's. "School tomorrow, I think," she said gently.

Reluctantly, Min nodded.

When she entered the classroom, braced for trouble, Mr. Harmon had finished with autobiographies and moved on to something entirely different. He seemed not to realize that one student had not done the assignment.

"What was wrong with you anyway?" Penny asked.

Min swallowed. "I don't know," she mumbled. It was true. She did not understand it. Something deep inside her still hurt whenever she thought of her "Life Story" being what the teacher had called "a rich tapestry." Hers was blank at the one end and dark and ugly since. And she wanted it to stay hidden.

She had read *Adam and Eve and Pinch-Me* during her week off, though, and the foster children in it comforted her somehow. The main character was older and shut herself off from people much as Min had done before Jess came along. And the dogs had comforted her, even though Emily was still distant. She's like me, Min had thought. Cassie had papers saying she was a pedigreed Peke. But Min had nothing. No birth certificate. No baby pictures. No grandparents with stories to share. Nobody to interview. Not even a real birthday. They had given her the date she was found, not seeming to realize it was also the day she was lost. Min the mutt, she had thought, looking back. Then she had lifted Emily onto her lap and driven Cassie crazy by giving Emily extra petting.

She decided to confess to Jess that she had told Penny and Jennifer that she was adopted, but when she tried to think up how to start, she could not find the words. Even though it still hung over her like a black thundercloud, the punishing storm never arrived. She kept on, day after day, carrying the weight of her guilty secret.

Slowly the anger within her began to drain away. Bit by bit, she, like Emily, could just go inside herself for a while and then come out again, feeling more and more whole.

Ms. Spinelli came back at the end of the first week in February and the concert began to take on more reality. One night Toby came for supper and told them about people trying to match up babies and toddlers with their parents after the tsunami.

"Two women fought over one baby," he said, through a mouthful of salad. "They're going to have to do a DNA test to settle it. I wonder what they would have done before they knew about DNA."

"You know the Bible story about Solomon and the two

women who claimed one baby was theirs, don't you?" Jess said.

"Oh, yeah," Toby said, grinning. "I wonder if that would have worked."

"What story?" Min asked.

Jess found the place in the Bible and read it aloud. When two women each claimed a baby was hers, King Solomon ordered that the child be cut in two so each woman could have half. The woman who was not his mother agreed to this at once, but the real mother cried out that the other woman could take him, rather than have her son killed. So Solomon decreed she was, in fact, the baby's mother.

Min stared at the open Bible and thought about the story. Then she raised troubled eyes to Jess's face.

"I think, even if I had been the one who wasn't his mother, I wouldn't have wanted him to be cut in two," she said, her voice low. "I don't think anyone who wasn't totally crazy could bear to see something so terrible done to a baby. Shirl cut off my hair and I thought she was trying to kill me, but I figured it out when I was older. What she was really doing was disguising me to keep me safe. She shouldn't have left me the way she did, but even Shirl …"

Her voice trailed away. Jess looked at her and Min saw sudden tears come into her eyes.

"You're right," she said, her voice more than usually husky. "I have always thought that there was something wrong with that Bible story, but it took you to show me what. I think you're right about Shirl too."

"She was the one who left you in that washroom, right?" Toby demanded, his face hard.

Min nodded.

"Well, I think she was wicked and heartless and I don't care what you say in her defense. Anybody could have picked you up. And she didn't even hang around to make sure you were safe before she took off," he said, his voice as unyielding as iron.

"No," Min said, thinking back to that day she longed to forget. "I kept looking for her."

As Jess put the Bible back on the shelf, Min remembered Shirl, laughing and wielding her long, sharp scissors. The steel blades had kept flashing with light reflected from the window and Min had been terrified, but had not dared to move in case Shirl lost her grip and plunged them into her bared neck. The memory made her grab hold of her braid and cling on until she could calm her suddenly ragged breathing. Toby was right. The little girl trailing through the Ex had been so alone and at the mercy of any passerby.

Toby was watching her. He looked away abruptly.

"What's for dessert?" he demanded in a loud voice, scattering the shadows.

"Fresh fruit," Jess said, keeping her face deadpan.

"And ice cream maybe?" Toby hinted, grinning.

"Ice cream maybe," Jess agreed.

Min jumped up to clear the table. Before coming to live with Jess, she had not cared much for ice cream. But this last foster mother of hers bought rich, fancy ice cream. It tasted like an entirely different food than the stuff Enid Bangs had served. She hoped it would be Pralines and Cream, even though she knew Toby liked Rocky Road better.

She opened the freezer and saw two containers.

"Hey, Tobe, double yum," shouted Min.

And she did not let herself think about lost babies again that night.

16

Bully Run

THE EXCITEMENT BUILDING as the date of the concert neared pushed Laird Bentham out of Min's mind. But two days later he turned up, horrible as ever. Min had seen him before, but had managed to avoid him, since they were in different homerooms. She had never told the others all the details of how he had tormented her over the years they had gone to the same school. She could not bring herself to admit the things he had said, the names he had called her and egged other boys into joining in. Girls had added their bit, too. Min had hoped he was gone from her life.

But she should have guessed it was not going to be that easy. When she came out onto the playground he was waiting, leaning against one of the trees, smiling his fat, nasty smile. It was a smile Min had learned to dread, but she did not see it at once.

Penny and Jennifer and Amy came out right behind her. They were all deep in a happy discussion of the concert.

Then his slimy voice called, "Hey, Minnie McDumpster. Do those girls know you were picked out of a garbage bin? Did you tell them you're trash?"

Min went rigid. She could not have moved if she had wanted to. She did her best to control her facial muscles, but her eyes burned and her knees shook. What could she say? What was Penny thinking?

Then Penny sprang into action. While Min had been home "sick," she had talked to her cousin, as she'd promised, and she was primed for action. She had told the others the plan, and she had started to explain it to Min over the phone once, but had been interrupted. Min had not quite understood it and had not thought of Laird since, what with getting ready for the concert. She looked at Penny now, trying to remember exactly what she had said.

"Let's shut his lying mouth," Penny shrieked to her friends. "Let's give him a dose of Bully Run."

Min felt Penny grab her arm and pull her own arm through it. In seconds the four girls were joined in a line, their elbows linked. And here came Sadie and Hannah.

"Bully RUN!" Penny began to shout, as they advanced like a mighty army. "Bully RUN! Let's see the BULLY RUN."

Laird did his best to hold his ground and keep his sneer in place. But when a line of six girls came at him, moving as one, shouting something he could not quite make out, his nerve shattered and the sneer vanished from his face. He turned and fled. Glancing back over his shoulder, he saw them still coming, still chanting. And now there were eight of them and more latching on with every step. And they were laughing at him!

Min was the only one who was not yelling. She was too stunned. Friends were standing up for her. Even Sadie, who had not been in their class as long as Min. Even Gloria, the class beauty. Everyone was taunting Laird. He was running for his life. When he stumbled, they cheered.

"Need any help?" a boy's voice called.

"No way," shouted Penny. She was dancing around now, shrieking with glee as the boy who thought he was all-powerful tried to escape and went floundering into a snowbank.

"He's actually blubbering," Amy reported, peering after him.

Min snapped out of her trance and began to laugh too. She had never seen anything so wonderful as Laird Bentham fleeing with his face all red and tearful and with snot coming from his nose. Penny leaned down and scooped up a wet handful of snow and sent it flying after him. It landed in a sloppy smack on the back of his neck that sent the girls into fresh whoops of delight.

"What is the meaning of this?" a deep voice demanded.

It was Mr. Smithson, the Phys Ed teacher.

"Ask Laird, sir," Jennifer told him.

"We're teaching a bully not to mess with us in future," Penny said sweetly, dusting the snow off her mitts. "But we have not laid a hand on him, have we, you guys?"

"No," they chorused. "Didn't touch a hair of his head."

The teacher went after Laird, but he did not hurry.

"It was Penny's cousin's idea. I bet it'll work every time," Jennifer said. "I almost wish there were more evil boys around so we could do it again."

"But what if … ?" Min began, uncertain what she meant to ask.

"If he had a gang with him, you mean?" Penny asked. "Somebody would go for help then, I guess. But I don't think old Laird will be able to come up with a gang, not after Bully Run. My cousin says people who make friends with bullies usually follow after them because they are scared that if they don't, they'll be beaten up. Cowards, he says."

"I was always the one who ran before," Min whispered, her cheeks reddening with memories of her years of being publicly humiliated.

"You were alone, right? He's big and he's mean," Penny said scornfully. But bullies are usually pure mush inside. You only need some friends to help you stand up to them to scare the pants off them. My cousin Edward told me. If nobody is with you, get people and go for them next time. What a creep that Laird is!"

Min thought of how exultant she had felt watching him run. She supposed she should have pitied him, but he had never pitied her, not once. Now she was positive he would never mess with her again.

She hesitated before telling Jess what had happened, but finally she could not keep the jubilation to herself.

"Oh, the power and the glory!" Jess said. "Bravo for Penny. She sounds as though she's a great friend to have."

"Yep," Min said.

"Would you like me to speak to the principal about Laird?"

Min opened her mouth to say yes when she realized that Laird was in the principal's office day after day. She had seen him there, hunched over, on the bench where kids waited to be told off.

"If there's a next time," she said slowly, "but I think maybe my friends fixed him."

"Good," Jess said. "It's wise to fight your own battles whenever possible. You tell that Penny I think she's a wonder."

Min nodded. She stared at her hands, which were balled into fists in her lap. What would Jess have said if she had seen Min before, standing like a post, scared witless? Or fleeing down the street?

"When I got chased like that," Jess said quietly, but with the hint of a smile, "I used to wet my pants. In public!"

And Min knew she understood everything.

17

Rock-a-Bye, Baby

SUDDENLY IT WAS FEBRUARY and the concert was only days away. Penny and Min practiced their duet daily. Min wished she felt her singing was improving.

"You need to PROJECT, Min!" Penny's mother urged her. "Shy voices, however sweet, don't reach the ears of the audience."

"Maybe Penny should sing by herself," Min mumbled, scuffing her toe back and forth on the rug and not looking at the woman.

"No way!" Penny yelped. "I can't do it alone. Besides, Ms. Spinelli already has us down as a duet, you nut."

"You have a very nice voice, dear," Penny's mother said hastily. "And it is improving daily. Just try to throw it out at your listeners more."

Min felt like a pitcher who is about to be sent down to the minor leagues after having a tryout with the stars.

"Start again," their pianist ordered and began to play the opening bars. When they had sung it through twice more, she said," I'm sure it'll be fine on the night."

Maybe it would be, but Min had a sinking feeling that she might open her mouth and no sound whatsoever would emerge.

Every class in the school had become involved and most were performing. There were lullabies and silly songs and even rounds. The French teacher had them all singing a song in French and then Ms. Spinelli suggested that they insert three or four recitations.

"They've actually got my little brother doing 'Wynken, Blynken and Nod,' dressed in a nightshirt," Jennifer told them, trying hard not to giggle. "He looks like a cherub – which he definitely is not. Mum said she would murder any of us who laughed at him, and I think she means it."

Valentine's Day fell on a Monday so they had their last rehearsals on Thursday and Friday. Jess had a class on Friday, but she came to listen on the Thursday afternoon. She sat at the back and told them how Jessye Norman's mother had commanded her to "stand up straight and sing out." Min had no idea who Jessye Norman even was, until they played a CD of her singing spirituals that evening. Her voice filled the house with mellow sound and feeling too.

"Wow," Min murmured. "Penny and I don't sound a bit like that."

"I'm planning to sit at the very back on Monday," Jess said, "and I want to hear every word. If I can't, I'll stand up and shout, 'Sing out, Jessamyn and Penelope. Stand up and sing out.'"

Min giggled. "You *wouldn't,*" she said.

"Don't be too sure," Jess said, her eyes gleaming.

Min felt more and more anxious as the time neared. She sat on the floor stroking Emily. "Maybe we will both get braver soon," she said.

"Well, I have some good news about that little dog," Jess said. "I went out to see how Miss Hazlitt was doing. I wasn't going to say anything, just see if she was having troubles. And I found out she was leaving on the weekend for a month in Florida with her niece, who has rented a condo and has invited Miss Hazlitt to come along and have a rest from the snow. I told her that was wonderful and I did not tell her why. But I know she won't be home until over halfway through March. Stop grinning or I'll call you Minerva."

Min leaped up and began to dance, feeling as though a huge weight had been lifted off her shoulders. Emily shrank back and Jess laughed.

"Keep that up, young lady, and your rescued dog will be begging you to find her a safer place to hang out," she said.

Then the dreaded day of the concert arrived. Min peeped through the curtains and spotted Raymah and her sister Lisa in the second row. Then she saw Mrs. Willis. No Enid, thank goodness. Laura and Baxter were there with the Dittos, who waved wildly every time the curtain twitched. Toby was nowhere to be seen. She was about to give up on him, with a pang of disappointment, when she saw him sitting beside Jess at the very back.

"Let me have a turn, will you?" Pravda hissed and Min stepped back, satisfied that everyone she cared about was there. Now if only she could make her voice strong and sure — or even just audible!

Twenty minutes later, when she and Penny walked onto the stage, side by side, and looked over at Penny's mother and saw her wink at them, Min found herself actually excited. She was even looking forward to singing.

Remember the foundlings, she whispered to herself as the first chord sounded.

Then they had started, their voices blending, and she felt fine. As they reached the last wistful notes, she saw Jess, actually on her feet with both hands in the air, applauding like mad. Toby, beside her, was still seated and was hiding his face behind his two hands. Then he dropped them and grinned right at her.

Although Min knew, when they finished, that she was

never going to be the singer Penny was, she felt thoroughly pleased with her performance.

"Boy, am I glad that's over!" Penny exclaimed when they were safely backstage.

Min stared at her. "Didn't you have fun?" she asked.

Then it was Penny's turn to stare. "I was petrified," she said.

Jennifer's little brother brought the house down with his recitation. He really did look like an impish cherub.

When it was all over, and the money was counted, the students had raised over nine hundred dollars. The parents matched the amount and boosted it a bit so that two thousand dollars went from Victory School to help all the orphaned babies.

When they got home, Min wanted only to fall into her bed, but her attention was caught by what she saw on the wall on either side of the long mirror. On the left hung the framed Christmas tree picture she had given Jess. On the right, also beautifully framed, was her Rock-a-Bye, Baby poster.

"Oh, Jess, they look so … so …" she started.

But she could not find the right words.

"Professional," Jess said calmly. Then she added, with a twinkle, "To think I kidnapped you without ever suspecting I was getting myself such a gifted daughter."

Min blushed and then went to bed humming a song. The tune was from *Oliver!* but she made up new words that started, "Here is love."

18

The Trouble with Eavesdropping

"YOU KNOW WHAT, JESSAMYN," Jess said a few days after the concert, "I think we get along almost too well."

Min, who was busy drawing a picture of the dogs, was startled.

"What … ?" she began.

"Well, I read once that Anne Shirley is much too sunny to have gone through such an unhappy time before coming to live with the Cuthberts at Green Gables," she said. "The writer claimed that Anne showed no trauma, and she should have. But you and I are happy too. Maybe we are about due some trauma."

Min snorted and went back to her picture. Anne Shirley was a bit of a nut, she thought, always mixing up bottles. She was fun, though, and Min liked her being happy-go-lucky.

"If Anne were real –" Jess began again.

"She seemed real to me," Min said and held up her drawing for an opinion.

At the end of the first week in March, Jess told Min that Toby and his family would be coming over for supper on Saturday.

"It's the twins' birthday," she said. "Laura plans and runs the children's party and I put on a family dinner afterward. They'll be five this year. She's done a Year of the Horse theme for them at home, with a pair of those big, bouncy rocking horses on springs for presents, a cake with a horse on top and a bunch of horsey videos. I'll bet you're broken-hearted that you and I weren't invited."

Min laughed, but she felt a pang of disappointment too. She probably would have found it babyish, but she had never attended such a party. In all her several foster homes, she had somehow missed out on them and she herself had no idea what her own birth date was. The Children's Aid had given her August first, the date she was found. But, to Min, it was the date on which she was abandoned too, and she hated it. She had never felt it was a day to celebrate, although by the time she was old enough to have explained this to Mrs. Willis, she knew she would be invited to choose another one, and there was no other date she felt was special.

I don't even know if my mother bothered to take me home from the hospital, she thought bitterly. I'll bet she didn't.

As she helped set the table for the twins' dinner, Min felt a small seed of resentment take root inside her. She stamped it under and began to fold the special napkins. They had prancing ponies on them, she noticed. So Jess wasn't as scornful of Laura's decorations as she pretended.

She asked Jess if Grace and Margaret could be trusted not to terrorize Emily, and Jess said they definitely could not.

"Take Emily and her bed up to the attic. She can stay there until they've gone," she said. "We can hook that door shut – they aren't tall enough to undo it. We had it put in as soon as they began to toddle around."

Emily struggled, but once she was put in her own bed, she settled down and lay still.

"I'll come for you the moment they go," Min promised and went back down.

Everything went as well as could be expected. The little girls, in ruffled dresses, were smiled at and fussed over. The rocking horses had been an enormous success, although Laura claimed that, if she had known they neighed, she would have looked for something quieter.

"They make a racket when they are bouncing backwards and forwards too," Baxter remarked, gazing at his lovely but noisy daughters. The twins ignored this and continued to make a huge mess of the table, spilling juice and mushing up the devilled eggs they were supposed to adore.

"Min and Toby will clear away the dishes and bring in the dessert," Jess said. "You'd better stay on your chairs, girls, if you want some ice cream."

Grace and Margaret, who had been sliding under the table, scrambled back up and resumed their angel faces. They spilled ice cream and they crumbled cake. Nobody said a cross word to them. Min, who could tell they were being bad on purpose to embarrass their parents, longed to smack them, but knew she would never be forgiven.

"Maggot is *so* bad," Grace said after Margaret dipped her finger in the chocolate syrup and tried to draw on the tablecloth with it.

Everyone but Min laughed.

After the candles were blown out and the feasting was over, Toby and his stepfather drove the twins, kicking and screaming, home to their babysitter, and went on to attend a peaceful basketball game. Min was left at home with Laura and Jess.

"Let's go and gab in the living room," Jess said to her friend. "Min can deal with this mess."

Min did not mind usually. She knew how to operate the dishwasher, and the dishes they had used for the first course were already in the kitchen. She would only have to clear away the ice cream bowls and cake plates.

But she caught the look Toby's mother shot at her, as though she had doubts about trusting Min with the job. She also did not like the way Jess had announced she would take care of things. As though there was no need to say please, no need to ask.

Now I'm a scullery maid, she thought, like poor Becky in *A Little Princess*. Ever since she had read the book last year, she had felt Becky and she were fellow sufferers.

As the women left, she began to clear away the dessert bowls, making as much noise as she dared. Then she remembered Emily shut upstairs. Leaving the dishes half stacked, she climbed to the attic. Emily looked pleased to see her. Min lifted her out of the small fleece-lined bed and ran down to Jess's room with it. An instant later, she was back to collect Emily before she could panic. The little dog was so relieved to see her that she did not even struggle to jump out of Min's arms, but licked her ear fondly on their way down the stairs.

Min left her back in the bed. Putting off the dishwashing job a few minutes longer, she tiptoed up the hall to check on Cassie, who had been asleep in Min's room after fleeing from the Dittos' overly rough petting. She moved as quietly as she could, not wanting to interrupt the women gossiping.

As she neared the door into the living room, she stopped short. She had just heard Laura's cool voice say, "I still don't understand what made you take in that girl, Jess. I remember clearly that you said you had no intention of adopting a baby after Greg died. If you wanted household help –"

"Min is not here to give me household help," Jess snapped. "Neither is she a baby, in case you haven't noticed.

Min did not want to eavesdrop on this conversation but, as she eased backwards, she could not help catching the next few words.

"I know her story," Laura said frostily. "Tobias is up in arms about it. But it still seems risky. You know nothing about her background."

"You sound just like Mrs. Lynde in *Anne of Green Gables*," Jess said, decidedly annoyed now. "Next thing you'll be telling me she'll murder us all in our beds, too."

Min stood in the shadowy hall fighting for breath. Then she silently opened her bedroom door, slid through, closed it behind her as soundlessly as she could and lay face down on the bed.

"I won't clean up their mess," she hissed into Cassie's sympathetic ear. "I won't and she can't make me. I hate that Laura. I'm not Jess's slave. I am tired and I didn't invite them over. I don't feel like cleaning up after such brats. Why should I?"

She lay curled into a ball, silently fuming at everyone she knew. A few minutes later she heard the two women laugh and she was positive they were laughing at her. She gritted her teeth and waited for Laura to leave. Finally, she heard the front door open and Jess calling farewell. She turned her back to the door and closed her eyes tightly. Let Jess come in and check. She, Min, would be sleeping.

Jess knocked softly.

Min did not stir. Cassie gave a short yip, but hushed.

Jess opened the door a crack, peered in and without speaking or coming in further, closed it quietly.

Min still did not move hand or foot but she strained her ears. What would Jess do next? Time crawled by. There was no clink of dishes, no whir of the dishwasher. She sneaked a quick look at her watch and went on waiting. At eleven o'clock, feeling her eyelids growing heavy, she could not stand it another minute. She slipped out her door and peered across the hall into the living room.

Jess was sitting in her reclining chair, still fully dressed, and she appeared to be sound asleep.

Min stood and stared at her. Was she faking – the way Min herself had done earlier? Apparently not. After another full minute, Min tiptoed down the hall. The dirty dessert dishes still sat on the dining table just where she had left them.

Moving without a sound, Min carried them out to the kitchen. Then she loaded the dishwasher. She put in the detergent. She almost turned it on and decided the noise would wake Jess. She went back to check on her.

The reclining chair was empty. Min stood stock still and stared at it for a long moment. Then she went back down the hall to Jess's bedroom door and opened it a crack. Jess was in bed. Her back was turned to the door. Min could have sworn she was not asleep, but she was doing a good imitation, breathing deeply and evenly. Then she gave a gentle snore.

That snore was definitely phony.

Choking with laughter, Min backed out and took herself to bed. She was asleep again before she had a chance to think the evening over. The only thing she noticed was that she had stopped being mad.

She woke when Jess called her to breakfast. Min hesitated, then went down the hall to face her foster mother.

"Good morning, Jessamyn," Jess said.

Their eyes met.

And, the next instant, they were collapsing in a fit of mutual laughter.

"But I am *not* household help!" Min got out.

"That's what I told Laura," Jess said. "But you were, you know! Thank you so much. You worked like a Trojan – and so silently."

And the hug she gave Min made up for everything.

A little later, as they ate, Jess said in a voice that was both serious and amused, "Do you think we've done it now?"

Min took a spoonful of raspberry jam and then looked up. "Done what?"

"That trauma we were failing to have?"

Min put down her knife and stared straight at her. "Maybe," she said steadily, "but Laura doesn't like me – and I am not keen on her either."

"Laura gets mad at me too. She feels I somehow stole her baby from her, even though she did not want him at the time. I suppose she now thinks you might be stealing me from Toby. Oh, who knows? She's not an easy friend to have. But, prickly or not, I'm stuck with her unless I want to lose Toby."

Jess's voice halted. Min bit into the toast while she thought over what she had just heard. She found she knew exactly what Jess meant. She didn't want to lose Toby either.

"I guess we're both stuck with her then," she said quietly.

Jess rose and leaned over to give her a swift hug. Her words, when they came, were husky.

"Bless you, my Min," she said.

19

Dancing Through the Snow

MARCH WAS ALMOST OVER when Jess mentioned, in a quiet, steady voice, that Emily was looking much better.

"While you were at school, I took her to see Jack," she said, reaching to stroke the little dog curled up next to her chair. "She weighs almost ten pounds now and her mouth is healed. No more colitis. She's eating like a regular dog too. I actually offered her a bite of egg this morning and she gobbled it down."

Min stared out the window and said nothing. She knew what Jess meant. She had been expecting it. But she wasn't ready.

"She's still strange," she got out after a couple of minutes had crawled by.

"Perhaps she always will be," Jess said. "But she is very lovable, isn't she? It's up to you, Min. You found her and it is because of you that she's well now. But you do have Cassie and I think Miss Hazlitt is lonely. She would doubtless deny it, but that is my guess."

"What if Emily ran out again and got caught by those people or by a coyote … ?"

"I thought we could make sure that Miss Hazlitt's backyard is fenced to keep Em safe. You think about it, honey. There's no rush. Remember, Miss Hazlitt still has no idea we have her."

Min thought about Cassie suddenly. What if her darling Cass was lost and, instead of returning her, the people who found her kept her? She loved Emily, but Cassie was hers in a way Emily had never been. Cassie knew Min was her person.

Did Emily feel that way about the old lady?

Min remembered how Miss Hazlitt's voice had cracked when she spoke about Daisy. She knew then that it was settled. Daisy was going back.

They called to make sure Miss Hazlitt would be home the following day. Toby wanted to come. When he told his family, the twins begged to be included.

"Definitely not," Toby said.

"I think not," Jess said when he told them. "It's going to be stressful enough without their shenanigans."

Min wondered if it was really settled, but hoped for the best. Then Laura called Jess to ask if she could possibly take the little girls for the afternoon because she had been invited to go to a book club. Min could hear her voice, sweet as pie.

"I can't think what the fuss is all about, but whatever you are planning, they are dying to be included. And their regular babysitter is away, I'm afraid. I can stay home, of course, but …" Jess sighed and gave in.

"I know when I'm beaten," she told Toby and Min, who were watching her with accusing eyes.

"How did the twins find out?" Min asked.

Toby growled that trying to keep anything secret at his house was absolutely impossible. "They eavesdrop," he said as though that were the worst sin he could think of.

Min's eyes met Jess's and they both smiled.

Jess went on to say she thought maybe Laura really did need a break.

"Miss Hazlitt enjoys children," she added, grinning at their matching scowls. "And you've told her so much about the twins' exploits. It'll be fine, you'll see."

Min got out of the van and began to carry Emily to the cottage, with Cassie trotting at her heels. Toby followed her, leaving Grace and Margaret playing outside for the moment.

"Remember," Jess said, "you promised to do as you are told. Toby will come and fetch you when it's time."

When the door opened, the old lady stared at the fluffy little dog cradled in Min's arms. She did not speak until she had reseated herself in her armchair.

"That looks like Daisy," she said then, in a voice that was

almost a whisper. "At least, her face does. Daisy was mostly bones."

Min took a deep breath and squared her shoulders. She looked at Jess and then at Toby, who had picked up Cassie and now held her fast against his chest. Cassie was given to fits of jealousy when Min showed too much fondness for Lady Emily.

Finally, Min burst out with the speech she had been rehearsing inside her head all the way there. "She is your Daisy," she whispered, unable to speak aloud and keep her voice steady. "She never meant to leave you. She's just beginning to learn the world is a good place ... and you ... you were her first teacher."

She stepped forward and put the quivering dog down on the old lady's lap. Emily astonished everyone by tucking her head under Miss Hazlitt's arm and wagging her tail like a wildly excited feather duster.

"Look at her! She's so happy," Jess said, trying to be brisk, and failing. "And she has done a great good work with all her suffering – she has led the authorities to clean up that ... that miserable hole where she lived at first."

"Oh, Daisy ... " Miss Hazlitt said, her voice husky with tears.

"I'm sorry to have to tell you this," Toby broke in, his tone low and ominous, "but the Dittos are advancing. I heard them plan their strategy. They are going to claim to have frostbite from having to stay out in the cold. Shall I try to turn them back? It's like attempting to reverse Niagara Falls, but I'll give it my best shot if you say so."

Shrieks sounded outside the cottage door. Emily burrowed deeper into the wide chair so that only the tip of her tail end was visible. It no longer waved so joyfully and she had begun to tremble.

"Oh, the poor darlings, let them in," Miss Hazlitt said, all smiles. She had not yet met Grace and Margaret, only heard tales of their wickedness.

She would soon see, Min thought.

"Tobe, put Cass down," she yelled. "She'll distract them for a minute at least."

Toby bent and released a frantic Cassie, who whipped around and raced to meet the twins, yapping bossily and letting herself be mauled in place of her timid friend.

Jess had gone out and now returned with a pot of six daffodil bulbs just coming into bloom.

"Spring is almost here," she said, "so we'll celebrate. All animals celebrate new families in spring."

But it wasn't quite spring yet.

Going home without Emily robbed the afternoon of most of its magic. For such a small, quiet dog who seldom stirred, her absence left an enormous hole in their lives. For Emily it was a happy ending, and they kept telling one another so. But Cassie searched for her often and watched for her return at the front window whenever Min was absent. Even Jess kept reaching down her hand to stroke the soft ears and looking bereft when her fingers found only space. Only Miss Maude Motley seemed untroubled at the disappearance of Lady Emily.

"Don't you miss her, Maude?" Min asked.

Maude purred and licked her whiskers and kept her feelings to herself.

"I don't think there is such a beast as a sentimental cat," Jess said, looking down at her. "Never mind. Hard hearts are restful. No need to mop up Maudie's tears."

Min laughed, but all the while she was fighting to quell a fear that had crept into her heart. Jess had made that solemn promise. But what if Jess found another foundling, someone needing her desperately?

Ask her, she told herself. *Why not just ask her outright?*

But she couldn't risk it.

The weather began to warm a little and the wind had the smell of earth and growing things. Then, in April, fresh snow fell. Everyone groaned as usual, everybody but Min. She stared out the front window at the starry flakes swirling down, and smiled.

It had been snowing just like this the day she had gazed up at the family statue in the square and, minutes later, had snatched Grace before she dashed out into traffic. It was snowing still when Jess had kidnapped her and taken her home and she had had her first real Christmas.

Standing at the window, watching the feathery flakes drifting down, she remembered the limp paper snowflakes taped up on the wall of the waiting room outside Mrs. Willis's office. Some of them had looked so pathetic. She had still never tried to make one. She should.

She went to the dining room and pulled open the drawer where she and Jess kept art supplies, and dug out some tissue paper and a pair of sharp scissors. Sitting down at the big dining table, she started folding the paper the way she thought she had seen a woman doing it on television. Then, concentrating so hard she chewed her tongue, she carefully cut through the thicknesses of white. When she had made diamond-shaped holes and triangles and half a ring of what might be daisy petals, she put the scissors down and unfolded what she had created. Her snowflake was perfect.

"Up, up and away," she whispered, tossing it lightly into the air. It floated slowly down, turning as it fell.

"Wow!" Toby said from behind her.

Min whirled to face him. She had not heard him come in. Having no idea how changed her expression was from the sullen scowl she had worn when they were first introduced, she was mystified by his wondering stare. But she was too pleased with herself to waste time puzzling out its meaning.

"Neat, isn't it?" she said with delight. "I've never made one before."

"It's cool," he said, "but if you want to please the Dittos you'll have to learn how to make rows of joined children. Here. I'll show you."

She watched while he folded and snipped and then strung them out, a lineup of little paper girls holding hands and pointing their toes in a dancing row.

"Wow!" Min said, echoing his praise.

Then she laughed and carried the row of cut-outs to the steamed-up window pane. She pressed them against the wet surface so they stuck. The dancers stepped across the window in a festive line.

"Dancing through the snow," she said.

Toby laughed.

"They won't stay. You'll have to use tape when the glass dries," he said. "By the way, Jess has invited me to dinner. She's all excited about celebrating something, but she wouldn't tell me the reason. Is it your birthday or what?"

Min looked at him, wondering if he was teasing, or if he had forgotten that she had no idea when her real birthday was. But before she could decide, they both heard the front door open and Jess and Sybil Willis came in, shedding their boots and coats as they greeted Cassie and Maude.

"What's the big celebration all about?" Toby demanded.

Jess looked at him and shook her head. "You wait until Min and I have a chance to talk. We won't be ready for fireworks until she's heard my news and given her verdict."

Min wanted to show off her paper snowflake, but

something in Jess's words made her hesitate. If she had not known better, she would have thought Jess was feeling shy. Nervous even. She closed the scissors and dropped them into her patch pocket.

"In here," Jess said, leading the way into the front room. Then she turned on the gas fire and sat down beside it. She seemed not only shy, but speechless.

Mrs. Willis seated herself quietly on the couch and Toby, his gaze moving from face to face, settled next to her.

Min stood for a moment, her breath stopping and then starting up again. Then she perched on the edge of the rocking chair. Without being aware of what she did, she kept the chair still by bracing her right foot against the floor. Her dark eyes searched Jess's face for a hint of what was coming. The silence felt momentous.

They all waited for Jess to break it and explain. Suddenly, words spilled out of Jessica Hart's mouth, shaking words, excited and tumbling on top of each other.

"I want to adopt you, Min, if you are willing. You are my foster daughter now and you will go on being that even if you choose not to be legally adopted, but I want you to be my own girl, one that nobody can steal away."

Min stared at her, stupefied by what she thought she had heard. Could she be mistaken? Could the lie she had told Penny not be a lie after all? Was her deepest secret wish going to come true?

"Your new name would be Jessamyn Randall Hart, but,

needless to say, you would still be Min." Jess stopped to clear her throat. Then she blurted, "What do you say? Oh, Min, will we do it?"

Min still stared at her, but her breath quickened and her dark eyes widened and shone.

"Are you serious?" she croaked at last.

"I am," Jess said, laughing. "One does not joke about acquiring legal, lifelong daughters. I had to do a lot of talking and filling out forms to get this process started. I may have begun by snatching you from Sybil's office, but they won't let me get away with no red tape twice. Miracles take some doing, I'll have you know. But it is still up to you, Min. Maybe you should take time to think it over. There's no rush. It's a big step." The tremble in her rapid-fire voice denied her sensible words. Her cheeks were flushed and her hands, clutching some papers, shook.

Min grinned at her. She stood up and took a step toward Jess, as though to give her an enormous hug. Then she spun around instead and fled down the hall, through the kitchen and along the narrow hall into the bathroom, slamming the door behind her.

"What on earth?" Sybil Willis said, looking startled. "Shall I go … ?"

"Don't you dare move," Jess Hart told her. "Don't speak either. Just wait and see what she's up to. I'll bet it will be totally unexpected. You can trust our girl to do something spectacular."

Then they heard rapid footsteps approaching. A girl nobody recognized at first appeared in the living room door and danced over to Sybil Willis.

"Here you are, dear Mrs. Willis," Min said shakily. "I don't need this to hang onto any longer. I know who I am. I have a last name now and a real mother."

Then Jessamyn Randall Hart dropped, into her caseworker's lap, the long, thick braid that had been her anchor for so long, and threw herself into Jess's waiting arms.